MURDER MOST CONVENIENT

A MRS. XAVIER STAYTON MYSTERY

Robert Colton

This is a work of fiction. All of the characters and events in this story are fictional or used fictitiously.

For more information:
www.robertcolton.com

IN MEMORY OF
RUBY BRIGHTWELL

"We also know that he could not have been concealed in the room, as there is no concealment possible."

-Sir Arthur Conan Doyle

Also By Robert Colton

Rome to Alexandria:
A Collection of Short Stories

Pompeii:
A Tale of Murder in Ancient Rome

Pompeii:
A Conspiracy Among Friends

Pompeii:
Hazard at Bay

Pompeii:
Pluto's Maze

June 18, 1927

Dear Mr. Harland Orenstein,

Greetings to you on this day. As I am not sure the proper form, I shall come straightaway to the point of this letter. I understand that you are the agent for that famous novelist who writes the mystery books. After her recent mental breakdown, it has occurred to me that her writing career may be at a standstill. Furthermore, this would leave you with one less client. I am pleased to offer you my work.

I set myself upon the task of writing a splendid whodunit. Traveling to the country estate owned by my late husband's family, I was ready to soak in the atmosphere and listen to my muse tell me a story of deceit and murder. Instead, a crime actually happened, right before my eyes. I just wasn't able to see it.

I have written the story as it occurred, omitting few details. I understand that publishers trim the fat, so I shall leave that to the trained eye. At places within the text, I have left notes to you and your publishers that will need to be edited as well. I have also left unimportant characters unnamed as of yet.

My business manager would not approve of my frankness, but I must add that I am a wealthy young woman; my writing endeavor is not for the purpose of profit or to gain fame. My goal is that, with publishing my work, I might dedicate it to my dear husband's name.

You will find the manuscript enclosed. I do so hope that it meets with your enthusiastic approval.

Most Sincerely,
Mrs. Xavier Stayton

Chapter One

Lucy had her nose tucked into her book so deep she didn't even notice me step into the sitting room.

"What are you reading so intently?" I inquired.

My bright-eyed friend mumbled, "A mystery."

Mimicking her wonderful English accent that I so envied, I repeated her. "A mystery."

My terrible attempt to sound like a local caused Lucy to laugh. I coveted the sound of her chuckle as well. It was so very "British." When I laughed, I sounded as if I hailed from the American Midwest, which, of course, I did.

Lucy and I had been friends for these past three years, after we met at my husband's wake. My poor dear Xavier and I had only been married for eleven months, two weeks, three days, and two hours before a most terrible accident placed him in Heaven.

At the wake, I had recognized no more than a dozen attendees dressed in black, who were condoling me, the young widowed bride. I noticed that a fellow who worked for the funeral director seemed to be harassing a little woman my age, who looked quite fearful.

She was a pretty, petite thing, with dark hair and porcelain skin. If I lacked self-confidence, she would be the type of girl I'd avoid. My own appearance is decidedly *un-unique*. When inspecting my amber hair, medium brown eyes, and little pink lips, my father's friends would nod, smile, and tell me that I looked "sweet."

I made my way to where the mortuary staff member spoke in a hushed tone to the fretful young lady, and he explained that she did not know the family at all; she had merely attended the wake so that she might make a dinner out of the finger food being served by the wait staff. He had seen her doing the same at three other wakes over the past few weeks.

"Is this true?" I asked, aghast.

"It is. I do you peg your pardon," Lucy responded in her lyrical voice.

"But why?" I inquired, although I already knew the reason and regretted blurting out the words. Her black shoes where scuffed, and one heel had been poorly repaired. She wore no jewelry, and one of her white gloves had been mended at the joint of the thumb and forefinger.

"I haven't the money to buy—"

I raised a finger to my lips and said, "I understand." Mimicking my privileged mother-in-law, I first shooed away the mortuary employee and then beckoned one of the maids. "Take my friend to my room; she's quite tired. See that a hardy plate of dinner is sent to her right away."

This was how our friendship began. For whatever divine purpose, Xavier had been taken away from me, and Lucy had been sent as my companion.

Mother Stayton thought nothing of Lucy staying on with us. At the funeral, she assumed that Lucy was a friend of mine whom she had yet to meet; she had no idea that Lucy was, in fact, a friend that I hadn't yet met myself.

I enjoyed a good book, but this tome in Lucy's hands had me perplexed. She had been reading it all morning with great interest. "Who is the novel by?"

Lucy whispered the author's name, as if responding to me might interrupt the events cast in ink upon the pages before her.

"The woman who staged that publicity stunt?"

"It wasn't a stunt; her husband left her for his..." dear Lucy whispered the next word, "mistress."

"Poppycock,"— oh how foolish I sounded speaking the local slang—she set out to make herself famous, and she succeeded."

Defending the author, Lucy replied. "She was already well known."

"Was she? Had you heard of her before she went missing for a week, her husband suspected of foul play?"

"Of course I had," Lucy retorted, but a second later her little face scrunched up rather prune-like as she realized she might have accidentally lied. "Well, I think her name was familiar to me."

I just nodded; my point had been proven. The individual might be an excellent writer, but she was also rather clever with publicity.

According to the papers, the author's husband had left her for another woman. Seemingly, she then vanished, her car found abandoned. This created quite the sensation.

Over a full week passed before she was spotted at one of those hydropathic hotels, checked in under an assumed name. The papers said she had amnesia; she suffered some sort of breakdown. (I do realize that this digression may need to be edited, and I am open

10

to the suggestion of different wording. As you do still represent this person, you may prefer to omit any reference.)

I asked Lucy, "Tell me, why is this French detective of hers so unique?"

Delighted to explain, Lucy stuck her thumb in the book and partially closed it. After correcting me on his nationality, she said, "He notices everything—every detail; he is quite charming, too."

I sat on the edge of the chair beside my friend. Rolling my eyes, I remarked, "Tall, handsome, suave..."

Lucy described the man, who was not what I expected, and I threw my head back and smiled. "He's no Roman Novarro."

"Dear me, no," Lucy replied.

We both laughed, true mirth between friends, not those awful polite chuckles that people force when they have no response to someone's statement.

"Well, I don't understand the appeal," I told her.

Lucy grew quite serious and said, "No, you wouldn't; you read all of those American books."

"What American books?"

"You know the sort, about the Old West and Indians," she replied earnestly.

"I have read no such thing, thank you."

Lucy's brow rose, and her lips pinched; clearly she didn't believe me, and why should she? There was a stack of those books in my room, still on the dresser where my dear Xavier had left them—unread.

There was a brief silence; Lucy had read the expression on my face. She had realized the novels belonged to the handsome young man whose many photos crowded my mantel.

I reached across the side table and opened a little ceramic box. Plucking out a clove, I placed it gently on my tongue and savored the flavor.

The little spell of melancholy passed, and I asked her to read from the book aloud. I wanted to hear this master sleuth at work.

Lucy read one chapter to me, in her lovely voice. The little detective was ever so ingenious. Or should I say, his creator was a master of her trade. Planting all those misleading clues, with the actual important information just being mentioned on the surface. Yes, quite clever.

I took the novel from Lucy's hands and thumbed through the object. A book, one of the most marvelous things ever created. The thought occurred to me, *What if I wrote a book?* I turned back to the dedication page and imagined the words *To My Beloved Xavier Stayton*, and I was decided.

My mother had not been pleased with my decision to keep London as my home. She wanted me to move back to St. Louis and find another husband. On my last visit she had lost her ability to hold her tongue.

"I don't know why you continue to live with *that* woman!" Mother had snapped.

"She's my mother-in-law."

"She *was* your mother-in-law," came the ugly correction.

I gave Mother a raised brow that told her, *You've crossed a line,* and said, "You have two sons, each with wives and children. I am all she has."

I would never tell my insistent parent that Mother Stayton was dependent on me. Xavier's father had left her very little in his will; he planned on his son living

12

a long life, and so had bequeathed his estate to my husband. Mother Stayton and I never spoke of this. While the house and other property were mine, we called it all hers, as it had formerly been. This just seemed the right thing to do.

To my mother's distress, the pursuit of another husband never crossed my mind. I still had a husband; he just was no longer on this mortal plane. However, he was in my heart, and always in my thoughts.

"Look at you—your beautiful amber hair, those sparkling copper eyes of yours, and somehow you've managed to keep your little figure despite all those European chocolates. Do you plan on remaining a widow your entire life?" Mother asked, fearful of my reply.

"Xavier has only been gone for two years; how could I do that to him?"

My Great Aunt Dotty, sharing our company, voiced what I could not. She was rather senile and spoke without compunction. "Lucky man that husband of yours. You'll love him for the rest of your life. More men would be better off dying young, before their wives get to know them well enough not to miss them."

"Dotty, be silent. You loved Uncle Winston," my mother blustered.

Dotty cocked her shriveled head and replied, "For the first few years; then he became a bore. He was just a lot of hair in the wrong places and the constant smell of whiskey. I had to prick my earlobe just to put a tear on my face the day we buried him."

"Now, Dotty, that just isn't true; next, you'll be telling us that you pushed him down those stairs!" exclaimed Mother.

Dotty was either so far gone that she didn't mind admitting to murder, or her wits had kicked in and she was having a bit of fun. The old gal winked at me and said, "I never said that I didn't."

Of course, she was right. Xavier and I were just so smitten with each other before his death. He was still boyish, not quite a rough-and-tumble man yet. After he played cricket, in full dress, there was never the odor of sweat upon him, but rather a sweet musk that I shall never smell again. His eyes twinkled with excitement as he shared with me his adventurous daydreams, and his exuberant laugh was as innocent as a child's.

This was all I had to remember of him, his soft, gentle touch, as afraid of intimacy as I had been on our wedding night, his straightforward way of speech, his supreme love of life. We had no quarrels, never a rift between us, nothing to deter my loyalty toward him. My single complaint was that fretful secret of his, the secret that killed him.

When I departed from my parents' home, starting my journey back to Holland Park, Mother had whispered in my ear, "He was a fantastic young man, the perfect husband to you, and he'd want you to be happy."

I kissed Mother on the cheek and told her, "You are right." This gave her some hope that I would one day pursue another suitor. I felt a bit of guilt for giving her this false hope, but it was what she wanted. In fact, I was quite happy. Though brief as our time together was, Xavier had awakened me; he'd lit the candle that was my soul.

Here, I must state that Mother Stayton was particularly gracious to me. Xavier had set out to explore the entire world, only to return home two months later because he had found his true love in America. She would have been indebted to an ape if it had been the reason to end his conquest.

She had loved her son dearly; she had made him her entire life. Like me, she spoke of him as if he were still with us, just out of sight down the hall, but listening as best he could.

We got on fine in this way, and Lucy's presence aided us; she was that audience who was a member of the household but not family. We would hold back any unpleasant remarks; always agree with one another, as not to cause embarrassment.

With the new goal of writing a novel, I knew at once the prefect location to visit. I would need the aid of Mother Stayton to arrange for an invitation. I so hoped that she would see the merit in my request. (Now here is a good place for an experienced editor to help me. I am about to finish my digression on my relationship with my mother-in-law and lead back into the story just shortly after I left off.)

While Lucy and I had discussed my new goal of writing a novel, we had chosen to ignore the ruckus we heard brewing in the sunroom toward the back of the house.

As we approached, a familiar scene was playing out before us. The French doors to Mother Stayton's preferred location were closed.

Pawing at these doors was the family dog. This moody Airedale Terrier was referred to as *B.*

Xavier had explained to me that the dog had some lengthy breeder's name that his father could never manage to remember, and he had taken to calling the dog *Bugger* after becoming tongue-tied. He'd chuckled at this and told me the rest of the household simply called the dog *B* afterward.

Not knowing what this meant, I spent several days calling out, "Bugger! Come to me, Bugger." Finally, the little scrubby maid shushed me as I was summonsing the terrier, and she took me out to the gardener so that he could tell me the meaning of the word I'd been calling throughout the house.

Lucy and I stood next to *B*, and we watched the little pantomime through the glass doors. The butler and Clarice, the (careless) maid, appeared to be doing a strange modern dance, while Mother Stayton waved her embroidered handkerchief in the air.

I knew what else to look for, but it took a moment to spot the little creature.

"There's Toby!" exclaimed Lucy, pointing at the little blue parakeet atop a curtain rod.

Little Clarice climbed toward the bird, and found herself standing on the arm of the davenport. Knowing that the fearsome creature thrilled at the chance to land a good bite, Clarice slowly extended her hand toward the budgie.

As expected, Toby took flight just before he was grasped. The butler leapt for the escapee with no hope of capture, and then the flash of blue feathers did the only sensible thing: it flew back inside the open cage.

Mother Stayton collapsed to the divan and held her head in her hands. She was typically quite kind to the staff, but not to poor Clarice. The mousey little woman had broken too many items, stained too many fabrics, and misplaced too much correspondence.

This was not the first time Toby had been freed from his cage; Clarice had been changing his bathwater and had forgotten to close the little door. It would seem something similar had just occurred because Mother Stayton took great care of her little pet and would never have accidentally freed him.

Before the reprimand could be voiced, Clarice spotted us and flung the French doors open, overjoyed by the distraction Lucy and I would create. (This may need some editing; you see the dog had moved on because there was now no chance to catch the bird. I doubt this fact is important to my reader, unless they are curious as to why he did not follow us into the sunroom.)

Mother Stayton shot a disgusted look toward Clarice, who was, by now, quite immune to them. Her well-deserved termination might never happen. While technically my employee, I would never sack a domestic under Mother Stayton's direction. On the other hand, she would never fire a staff member on my payroll. Thus, unconcerned, Clarice and the butler straightened the room, which looked much like a crime scene.

As a girl, daydreaming of marriage, I had assumed my future mother-in-law would be an elder woman with grey hair and simple features. Mother Stayton defied this image.

Viviane Burk Stayton was a gorgeous lady. I did not know her age; I could only guess, based on the fact that her son was born in the year of nineteen hundred and four, that she was perhaps nearing the age of fifty.

Well-spoken, lovely in appearance, she made for quite the fashionable woman. I suspected she would soon remarry. A number of handsome chaps her age played escort to various dinners, theater performances, and the opera.

Xavier's father had died just three years before we met. Mother Stayton was fond of saying, "Mr.

Stayton died during the war." This was true, but he played no part in the war that I was aware of. He'd had a heart attack in his dressing gown while berating a cook about the healthy breakfast she'd prepared that morning.

While devoted to her husband during his life, I could not help notice how quickly her eyes landed upon a nice-looking fellow who might stroll past us in a restaurant.

These past seven years had been hard on her; she once remarked that a pretty woman looked best when matched beside a handsome man's shoulder. This had been said as I stood next to her son, but I think the comment was not directed toward me.

"You missed the bulk of the calamity. Clarice let Toby out—again," said Mother Stayton, waving me to sit next to her. "Oh, what is it that you are reading?"

"Actually, Lucy is reading it," I explained.

Sitting down on the chair across from us, Lucy said the book's name.

Mother Stayton's eyes opened wide. "Oh, one of those murder mysteries. Are you enjoying it?" She then looked over to the grey-faced butler, who was trying to scoop dirt from the floor back into a potted plant that had been overturned, and asked, "Did the butler do it?"

This member of the domestic staff had no sense of humor. Lucy and I both smiled at the comment, but we didn't encourage Mother Stayton to say more.

I cleared my throat, the surest way to indicate I had an announcement to share, and then said, "I have decided to write a book."

Mother Stayton clasped her hands together and said, "A writer! What a nice occupation for your time."

I believe that she was comforted by my embrace of widowhood. It was an honor to her beloved son that I should remain his, and only his, wife.

A queer expression crossed Lucy's lovely face. "What about the theatrical musical that you were writing?"

"As it turns out, my muse doesn't sing," I retorted.

Excited for me, Mother Stayton remarked, "She sleuths?"

"Indeed, and she has spoken."

Lucy wasn't one to leave a project half done, and with obvious disappointment, she said, "But you were so close to finishing your musical."

I had attempted to become a painter, but the brush was deaf to my desire. My piano lessons ended when my well-paid instructor commented that somehow, even when I managed to hit the right key, the note still sounded wrong.

I never understood poetry; some things were red, some things were blue, but this is as much as I can rhyme, and it only passes so much time.

My theatrical musical had kept me busy, but in my heart, I knew it was lacking. "Yes, Lucy, I have made great progress, but I'm always being set back when the scrubby maid pinches the bucket I carry all my notes in."

Lucy chuckled while Mother Stayton looked on, confused.

"No, a murder mystery, this shall be my calling." I turned to Mother Stayton. "You know how all the good ones take place at some stately country manor." She nodded, and I went on. "I thought perhaps I might pay a visit to your family in the county of Bedfordshire—soak up the atmosphere at their estate."

These were not, per se, *her* family; they were her late husband's cousins. I was putting her on the spot, but it would seem more fitting for her to send a letter asking that I might visit, rather than if I did so.

Mother Stayton seemed apprehensive and warned, "They come off all jolly and smiles, but they are queer people. Those same friendly smiles keep you from noticing the cold glare in their eyes." Her own eyes lost focus, as if she was recalling some ugly business with them, then returned, and she forced a little smile. "But then, they did adore my towheaded boy…"

Our eyes met, and I gave thanks to the Almighty that Lucy was in our company. Mother Stayton knew how this expression pained me.

The woman pressed her red lips together and lowered her lightly painted eyelids before she continued the conversation, the ugly moment past. "Of course, they are well-bred people; I'm sure they would treat you well."

Lucy and I smiled, staring the poor woman down like orphans who knew that her handbag was filled. with sugary candy. (Is that mean, to use orphans as a comparison? We do regularly donate a large sum to the local orphanage and send them presents from Father Christmas every year. Well, I'm agreeable to jotting down another phrase if it might be suggested by the editor.)

"I will send Cousin Nicholas a letter, baiting them to invite you." She looked me up and down and said, "We will need to take you shopping. They might live fifty miles away, but I dare say Joan knows what is currently displayed on each mannequin at H and N."

Chapter Two

As hoped, I received a flowery letter from Ruth Stayton, Cousin Nicholas's wife, inviting me to Pearce Manor for a week.

Lucy and I made our farewells to Mother Stayton, while two porters struggled with our baggage. My mother-in-law had instructed Clarice to fill the luggage with half of the spring line from her preferred department store.

Once onboard the train, the car attendant made a comment in French, accustomed to the well-bred English clientele recognizing this beautiful langue. Sadly, whatever he said sounded something like *la blabla, la gub-gub* to me. After all, I was still picking up the English spoken in London, a strangely different language than spoken in St. Louis.

There had been so many new words to learn. For example, when Xavier was explaining who was who among his family household, he told me, "Mr. Jack has managed the business affairs since Father died. Very good with numbers and records. Think nothing of his manners; he's a typical poof."

Upon meeting Mr. Jack, I told him I understood that he kept the financial affairs for the family, and thinking I had learned the British slang for accountant, I asked him how long he had been a poof.

As he blushed, his mouth gaping open without a sound, I thought to myself, *Well, he's a bit of Nancy boy, isn't he?*

Xavier said something clever to change the subject and then, once alone, he explained to me that Mr. Jack *was* a Nancy Boy. I was afraid to speak for the remainder of the week. (Now, should this be omitted? I would hate for Mr. Jack to be arrested and charged with homosexuality just based on household gossip and the fact that he always smells of lavender.)

Lucy took the train tickets from my hand, passed them to the attendant, and then replied in French. The fellow smiled and left us.

Settled in our seats for the brief journey, we mumbled polite greetings to the older couple who sat across from us.

I opened my handbag and placed it in my lap. After taking my gloves off, I retrieved my engagement and wedding rings from my purse. The engagement ring had belonged to Xavier's grandmother. The stone, a dazzling ruby, was too large to pull gloves over. This action caught the attention of the woman across from me.

Having been spotted ogling my jewelry, she had little choice but to remark, "What a lovely ring."

"Thank you. It belonged to my husband's grandmother."

The fellow gave my ruby a glance, and his eyes grew wide; then, a little frown passed across his face as he realized there would be some nagging comment once in private concerning his wife's slim, unadorned wedding band.

I gave introductions. "This is my dear friend, Miss Lucy Wallace. I am Mrs. Xavier Stayton."

They gave their names and started talking about the lovely spring weather. We were all jostled as the train made that initial lurch forward like a toddler either taking his first step or beginning another tumble. Lucy and the couple made that pleasant polite laugh that I so despise when there was no appropriate comment to be said, and I smiled and nodded my chin.

The sound of the whistle and rush of machine parts all astir were very loud, making conversation unnecessary. Once the train was some distance from the station, moving rather fast, we grew somewhat accustomed to the loudness.

Lucy leaned into me and pointed toward my purse. We both retrieved the little diaries we had selected while shopping for the needed supplies to write my whodunit.

My friend spoke just loud enough for me to hear her, in a very furtive manner, as if the plot of my novel were the most important secret. "Make a note of the car attendant. He was French; maybe something happened during the war and he can't return home, some sort of misdeed."

Yes, I scribbled this down before saying, "I was reading more on that Sherlock Holmes book last night and realized that my master detective will need a companion, some sort of assistant."

Lucy's forehead wrinkled. "Why?"

"The master detective needs someone to speak to, to make observations to. Otherwise, how does the reader know what the clues mean?" I explained.

Lucy's face lit up. "Oh, yes! He tells Watson his deductions, thusly telling the reader."

"Yes, you see."

"I hadn't puzzled that out before; you are already becoming the master detective." Lucy made a note on her pad. "Do you have a name for him?"

"No, it can't be a him," I remarked.

"No? Why?"

"My master sleuth is going to be a woman; thus her companion should be."

"A woman... Oh, yes! A sleek, elegant lady." Lucy became very excited. "She must say things like, *a ripping good time* and *scram, you pusher; you give me the heebie-jeebies.* Oh, and she should quote lines from jazz songs that relate to her cases."

Well, I wasn't sure about all that, but I smiled and nodded all the same. In truth, I had no choice but to write from the viewpoint of a woman; I didn't understand the point of view of a man. Xavier had been very modest. Never did I witness him clip his toenails, nor doing his morning stretches, these things I know that men do. In our brief time together, we had been rather shy, even as man and wife in the bedroom; there had been an air of innocence in our passions. (This may be too racy. Lucy had suggested some bit of *color* thrown in, but I am not certain that it is appropriate. Yes, I do think that it is telling that when Mother Stayton read this manuscript, I withheld this page.)

"Pearce Manor," Lucy said, followed by a sigh, her pencil ablaze with movement. "The name itself speaks of mystery."

The noise of the train was now very natural to us. The sound of chatter filled the railcar. Her interest piqued, the woman sitting across from us asked, "I beg your pardon, did you mention Pearce Manor?"

Not quite a social butterfly, Lucy froze for a moment rather than responding to the question.

Before anyone might be embarrassed, I said, "Yes, we are spending the week there. My husband's family resides at the manor."

"How very nice. Are you joining your husband there?" the woman asked ever so innocently.

That shadow crossed along my face; I could tell by how the pleasant couple gazed at me. "No, my husband died three years ago."

I was too young for anyone to suspect that I was a war widow. Why I mentioned how long ago Xavier found himself in Heaven with our Lord, I do not know.

"I'm so sorry for you; you are so very young," the woman replied. She knew that she should say no more, but she could not hold her tongue—they can never just hold their tongues. "What happened to such a young man?"

The expression on her husband's wrinkled face told me he momentarily considered stuffing his newspaper into his wife's open mouth.

"My dear Xavier was an explorer, you know the type. He was in Egypt with Mr. Howard Carter when they discovered that boy king's tomb. I'm sure you read about it in the papers." I reached into my handbag, pulled out a rabbit's foot, and clutched the little thing just below my chin.

The two of them were looking at me intently, their mouths held tightly shut, and their eyes open wide.

"I shouldn't say more, but, of course, you know about the curse…"

Their heads bobbed up and down.

"My poor Xavier was just the first." I then drew the sign of the Crucifix with my right finger and kissed my lucky rabbit's foot before whispering intentionally loudly, "But there have been so many more."

Dumbfound, both mumbled some sort of polite retort. Regaining his wits, the husband nudged his wife and said, "Is that Birdy Ralston over there, just at the front of the car?" and to me, "Do please excuse us for the moment."

I knew they would not return; they gathered everything they'd brought with them and escaped toward either their acquaintance, Mr. Ralston, or some poor stranger they would feel forced to strike up a conversation with so that if we glanced at them they could point and smile at the fellow.

Lucy made no comment about my silly lie. She had never asked me in which way the Lord had summonsed my Xavier. In the same manner, I had never asked her how she'd become poverty stricken and without family. We were a comfort to each other in regard to these unhappy happenings, and explanation was unnecessary.

Absent now the pair who might have learned my whodunit's plot, we settled ourselves. From the little silver snuff box in my purse, I took a clove and placed it on my tongue.

Lucy suggested. "You could model your characters from the household. Tell me about them."

I took a little breath and began, "I have only met them all twice, at the wedding and then the funeral. The elder brother and his wife, Randolph and Joan, sent us a nice gift; costly, I should say. This surprised Mother Stayton. She mentioned they had fallen on hard times. That is why they moved into Pearce Manor with his younger brother and sister-in-law. No sooner than she told me this, I opened Nicholas and Ruth's gift, and it was a small offering."

I recalled that Randolph had a bit of a cloud over his head from the war, but Mother Stayton was far too discreet to elaborate on the topic. It seemed best not to mention this to my cheerful companion.

Lucy penciled all of our insight into her journal. "Any correspondence with them?"

"Just the obligatory Christmas letter. Very dull, all trite."

"Each couple has children?" Lucy asked.

"Sons, both away at Eton."

Lucy's eyes twinkled. "College boys."

I rolled my eyes. "And then there's the staff, of course."

Lucy nodded. "A little short on characters. You need a vicar; they come in two varieties: the helpful, friendly ones who know a clue but don't realize it, and the mean, sour-faced ones who know the truth but won't tell."

"Brilliant." I jotted this down in my notebook.

The poor couple who had abandoned us couldn't decide if they should scramble off the train to avoid me, or hold back and wait until Lucy and I exited the car.

The French attendant made things easy on them. He stepped back through the open doorway and called, "Mrs. Xavier, a car awaits you."

Lucy and I looked out the window to see our baggage was already being wrestled in the direction as pointed to by a sharp-looking chauffeur.

The attendant directed us past other travelers, giving them the impression that Lucy and I were more important. I knew this meant I would need to place an adequate coin in the palm of the man's hand. How I wished he'd appreciate American currency; at least then I would know if I had given him the proper amount.

Gesturing to the driver, the Frenchman's deep bow suggested I had given him too much. No matter, Mr. Jack told me that I would have to try very hard to run through the fortune I had inherited. *Or open a line of credit for your good mother-in-law at H and N's,* he'd said with an effeminate harrumph.

The driver, courteous but not quite friendly, led us to a waiting sedan. A few bland statements of greeting and mention of the family's joy at our arrival were made before the man fell silent for the remainder of the journey.

Within the county of Bedfordshire, Bedford was a nice-sized town, but we saw little of it. Quickly, we were on the long, winding road that would take us to Pearce Manor.

Tall green trees lined the swerving lane, but otherwise, there was little to see. After taking a second hill rather fast, Lucy pointed at the radiator cap on the front of the motorcar. My eyes fixed on the winged angel I was unsure what Lucy meant until she giggled and said, "We are on a Rolls'er coaster." She giggled again at her silly joke, and I smiled and nodded my chin.

The trip by train hadn't taken a full hour. After twenty minutes in the car, which seemed to be sailing much more swiftly than the locomotive, I leaned forward and asked, "How much farther?"

"We are there now, ma'am." As the driver spoke, the car slowed, and a gatehouse appeared between a break of lovely hedges.

What had I imagined, a long, narrow lane, climbing steeply up toward something more like a castle than a home? Perhaps I had envisioned such a foreboding place because the cheerful lavender rhododendrons that lined the flat, straight driveway caused me to frown.

At the end of the colorful lane was Pearce Manor. I must admit that the place wasn't as grand as I had pictured. Three stories tall, made of a rectangular cut grey stone, there was something rather institutional about the place.

It was large, much larger than our home in Holland Park, but it wasn't the immense thing I had daydreamed of. There would be no suits of armor in a grand hall in this residence. This was a more modern affair, built little more than a hundred years ago, of that I was sure.

In contrast to the plainness of the home, I was delighted to see a little army of servants turned out along the walkway before the entrance.

The car came to a stop, and the driver quickly hopped out and opened my door. The servants bowed and then parted to reveal two well-dressed men, two lovely ladies, and one gaunt woman, who scowled at me with obvious contempt. These five people slowly walked down the steps toward us.

I had remembered them differently. At the wedding, I never matched the right names to right faces. At the funeral, everyone was just a dash of black clothing and sad faces. Other than the thin woman, whom I did not recognize, they were all quite colorful and youthful despite the fact that each couple had sons nearly my age.

They greeted me warmly, and then I introduced Lucy.

"So good to have you here. I am Nicholas Stayton. This is my wife, Ruth." Nicholas was tall, and in his youth, I imagine he had been gangly. His light brown

30

hair was oiled and parted to the side; he had small hazel-colored eyes, and the best way to describe his features is to say he looked very British.

Ruth, slightly tall, had sharp features; she reminded me of a bird of prey. All the same, she was very friendly as she reached for Lucy's little gloved hand and gave it a firm shake.

Next, Nicholas's older brother stepped forward. Randolph couldn't have been much past his mid-forties. He looked very much like his brother, with just a bit more weight on his frame.

"Oh, yes, our dear girl's friend Lucy; didn't we meet you at the wedding?" he said, sounding all too familiar and very shifty.

Lucy played it off well. She gave a little shrug and responded, "I don't recall."

An attractive platinum blonde glided between Lucy and Randolph, and I had the distinct impression that she made a habit of separating her husband from young women.

Taking Lucy's hand, she said, "I am Joan. Don't mind my husband; he recognizes every girl with a sweet face." In a pitch that edged toward sarcasm, she concluded, "They remind him of me in my youth."

Ruth forced that unnatural laugh that had nothing to do with humor, then she introduced the gaunt woman at her side, "This is Phyllis Masterson; she's like family to us."

As I have described Ruth as hawkish, how do I give detail to Phyllis? She had the darkest eyes I've ever seen. The pupils could not be discerned from the iris. Her short hair was jet black, died this color that rarely occurs in nature. Attired in a long grey dress, she appeared to be a charcoal sketch in contrast to those in lively watercolors beside her.

Nicholas seemed to recognize the timid smile I forced as Phyllis, in a begrudged fashion, took my hand with her limp, bony claw. "Right," he said, "well then, come on into the house."

Six wide stone steps led to the door, where a young male servant held the red leash of an apricot-colored Afghan hound.

Ruth stroked the dog's narrow head as she passed. "Nate is terrible with stairs."

"Do they even have stairs in Kabul?" said Joan, and the little group echoed their shared fake laughter, this being some inside joke. (I would later learn that the dog actually came from Kabul, a gift of the well-known breeder, but this information doesn't seem to fit into my story, nor does the jest seem any more amusing having explained it.)

Halfway up the wide stairs, I turned back to look at Nicholas, who had just winced. He seemed to have a bit of difficulty with the steps himself. "Are you all right?" I asked.

"Oh, fine. A bit of struggle with stairs," he said in a soothing manner.

Ruth added, "He was in an automobile accident; a drunk rammed into him."

Nicholas doubled his speed up the last two steps in way of playing down his injury and said merrily, "We are just a bunch of cripples at the old country manor, aren't we, Phyllis?"

I then noticed that Phyllis held her left arm, bent at the elbow, very rigidly under her slight bosom. The thin hand was clasped tightly, making a street boxer's fist.

Nicholas's comment brought about the first genuine smile I had seen on the pale woman's face. As Ruth and Joan scolded him, Phyllis said, "Indeed, we are, Mr. Nicky."

After winking at Phyllis, Nicholas stopped just as we were about to pass through the threshold of the two open doors. "Right. Now, then, Viviane told us in her letter that you had your heart set on writing one of those whodunits. I had the staff all turned out for you along the drive; that's how they do it in those books, isn't it? All proper and done up nice. Thought you would like the effect. I am afraid that's the best we can do. You'll have to use your imagination for the rest. We live a quiet life here in the country. No scandal, I'm afraid."

Famous last words, I thought to myself, as I said, "I do thank you for your kind hospitality. I'm just after the setting; my muse will tell me the rest."

They all gave me jolly smiles, but just as Mother Stayton had warned, the glare in their eyes was distinctively cold.

Ruth ushered me in, Phyllis at her side. I felt as if the grey lady was watching my face, expectant of something to happen.

Well, I was thunderstruck; passing through the vestibule, I felt as if I were stumbling into a French art gallery.

Ruth stretched her arms out and slowly spun a little half circle. "We just had it done; it is French modern art. I hear the term Art Deco is what it is being called..."

"Damned expensive is what I call it," Nicholas said with good humor.

Sounding almost suggestive, Randolph remarked, "The place looks like a woman's boudoir."

No, a nightclub, I thought. Where dark-stained wooden paneled walls had been, teal and peach Formica shined under a garish chrome and white glass chandelier. Modern art, the sort with faces done in geometric shapes, perched on these slick walls. In place of what should have been a large oak table with a marble top at the center of the grand foyer, was a black lacquer and chrome piece of furniture. Exotic flowers, not grown in any English country garden, stood from a rectangular mirrored vase.

The winding staircase, first leading to a landing on the second floor and then upward to a third floor, was completely covered in cream-colored carpet. The spindles of the banister were shiny black, and the hand rail was jade. All that was missing was the sound of a jazz band and the bustle of men in black tie and women in evening attire.

All I could manage to say was, "Lucy, have you ever seen such a place?"

She just shook her pretty little head; of course she hadn't.

Joan spoke, attempting to sound witty, "The French exhibition is limited to just these front rooms. There's still a natty couch or two and some real wood furniture the deeper you go."

Ruth ran her hand down Phyllis's good arm and said to me, "They all hate it, save Phyllis and I. We went to Paris last year, and I was quite taken with the style."

Without thought, words came out of my mouth, "It is lovely."

Phyllis's voice was as harsh as her appearance. "No, it is garish, but that is the intention."

"It has succeeded," Randolph quipped.

I felt an uncomfortable tension. It seemed these five people lived among each other in the same manner as a harem of Siamese fighting fish, nipping at one another when crossed.

Nicholas gestured to the porters carrying in our baggage and suggested, "I'm sure you would like to get to your rooms to freshen up."

Chapter Three

Lucy slipped into my room with her notebook and said in a whisper, "All that is missing is the vicar."

Our rooms were lovely. Filled with old bric-a-brac, heavy curtains, dark wood, all very English manor in appearance.

I was setting out my many photographs of Xavier on my vanity table. Lucy glanced at a photo and then to me, her smile a bit nervous. For here, I must say if I have not made it clear before, my dear husband had been a most handsome young man. These are not the words of a loyal and adoring wife, but a simple fact.

Despite my mother's opinion of me, I am no great beauty. Attractive enough, but my amber hair, kept at a fashionably short length, won't take to a permanent wave. My skin tone is neither light nor dark, and my eyes are an unremarkable shade of medium brown.

The unspoken question had always been, how did I manage to catch Xavier's eye, especially in that crowded dining room at Union Station? Well, I don't know the answer, but I thank the Good Lord every day that I did.

In reply to Lucy's jest, I said, "Is the vicar the sweet one or the sour one?"

Lucy was too kind to state that we seemed to have enough sour dispositions. She just scrunched up her little forehead and smiled.

I stepped near the window and gazed outside. A brilliant green lawn swept away some distance to a row of grand old tall trees. The afternoon sun was dazzling, and the blue sky looked nothing like the dusty haze that floated over London.

Lucy looked out, over my shoulder, and said, "It's very pretty, isn't it?"

"Too pretty. Where's the fog, and why isn't it raining? I was hoping for atmosphere," I lamented.

"Well, it is the middle of May," Lucy said apologetically.

I gave a great sigh and then turned to the writing table that had been put in the room for me. The new typewriter that Mr. Jack had ordered for us was already sitting on the desk. "Well, what do we have so far?"

Lucy opened her notepad and said, "A French domestic, unable to return to Paris because of some war crime."

I lost all reserve and retorted, "He could just go downstairs and find himself in Paris."

Lucy giggled and said, "The couple on the train, very sketchy, rushing off to rendezvous with Mr. Ralston."

"He didn't have a lipstick smudge on his color, nor she a missing earring," I remarked, implying they were boring.

I think Lucy was becoming fearful that my interest in writing would play out as well as my interests in painting, golf, or knitting had. "Your master sleuth, have you given her a name yet?" she asked.

I was still waiting for my muse to speak. "Not yet; for now, she is Miss X."

Lucy clapped her hands and said, "What a riot."

The significance was lost on me. "Why do you say that?"

She put a petite hand to her chin and made a little frown that somehow appeared jovial. "I guess you wouldn't know, would you? That's what the staff back home calls you, well, not Miss, but rather Mrs. X, short for—"

"Mrs. Xavier," I said in a faraway voice. A queer feeling passed over me, like when an angel whispers in your ear to tread carefully, and the person in front of you steps in a puddle. "Yes, Miss X."

Lucy did not perceive the wave of emotion that overtook me as I realized I had been quite destined to write my novel. She asked me, almost giddy, "What about Miss X's sidekick?"

I knew it would please her, so I suggested, "For now, let's call her Miss W."

Lucy's beautiful porcelain skin went flush with pink. "*W, X,* oh, that is rich."

"And so forth, we will call the victim *Y* and the culprit *Z*." I thought to myself, *Now I'm cooking with gas!*

***

We were called down to tea just as multiple chimes called out four o'clock. (Now, do I explain to my American readers that "Tea"—as it is called—refers to not only the beverage, but a light meal? In St. Louis this was not the custom. Of course, at the Plaza Hotel in New York they did put on a proper tea; maybe it is only in the Midwest we lacked this oddly timed light repast?)

38

Lucy and I had both changed our attire. Mother Stayton was counting on us to do her late husband's branch of the Stayton family proud.

It wasn't until we met atop the staircase that we realized that we were both in a variant of the same outfit. I with a little light green hat and matching gloves, Lucy in mauve. We both protested to change so the other would not need to, and then decided it would be a funny subject of conversation if we remained nearly twins.

Once seated side by side on a peach divan in the newly decorated drawing room, it was Joan who commented, "You two look like the cover of H and N's spring catalog."

Thankfully, Lucy did not take this as the insult it was meant to be. Rather spitefully, I silently reminded myself that Joan, the elder of the two cousins' wives had played witness to her husband fall on hard times. Her tongue had been sharpened by envy; I, the victim, had done nothing to incur her disdain.

Ruth sucked in her breath, as if a blasphemy had been uttered under her roof. She then said, "You two look quite pretty. We are all rather tweedy out here in the country. Mind you, we do still dress for dinner."

Nicholas remarked, "Satin after seven, as they say."

Ruth snapped her fingers to call the lovely dog to her side as she said in an almost guttural pitch, "No one says that, Nicky."

Nicholas smiled at me as he shrugged and rolled his eyes. *Yes, this was how they all spoke to each other,* I thought, and knew that our little trip would be filled with veiled insults that we were unaccustomed to.

Ruth poured the tea, and, as Lucy and I were guests, we were served first. Nervous servants stood at attention as we delicately picked at some of the little prim sandwiches on the tri-tiered silver stand.

Randolph then grabbed at several sandwiches of smoked salmon as his wife poured their own drinks. "Don't eat all of those; where are your manners?" Joan's hiss went ignored, as I'm sure it often did.

Nicholas, seemingly the most polite of the group, said, "Now tell us, dear, we've had so little chance to speak with you before, where about is Saint Louis? Is it closer to New York or Los Angeles?"

I took a sip of my tea to wash down the dry cucumber sandwich and said, "Actually, it is in the middle of those two cities."

Eyebrows were raised. I knew they thought I was a rube, but I didn't care. Nicholas asked, "So it is near Chicago, where all of the gangsters are?"

Joan barked out her harsh laugh, the fake sound that translated into the words, *You sound like an idiot.* "Nicky, I think they have gangsters all over America."

"Prohibition, what a dreadful idea," Randolph said, swirling his cup of tea as if it were a highball.

Ruth nodded her chin in agreement. "What does your family think of Prohibition?"

I gave a little shrug and replied, "Very little. My father has a man who keeps him stocked with whiskey."

Nicholas made a silly gasp, as if he was shocked. "Isn't your father a doctor? Couldn't he lose his medical license for such an offense?"

"I doubt that. The chief of police would have to explain why he frequents our home so often and never suspected my father of illegal activity."

This produced the polite chuckles that I anticipated, which were quickly broken by the sound of Ruth's voice, "Dear Phyllis, there you are. We started without you."

The grey lady pressed her lips together, making an imitation of a smile. She seemed to absorb a bit of the light from the festive art deco-inspired room.

Ruth turned toward her friend and said, "We were just hearing all about Prohibition." She waited for Phyllis to take what must have been her normal seat and went on to say, "What a shame we didn't make it to that speakeasy Fredrick told us about in New York."

Nicholas chimed in, "I hear what they serve at those places will cause blindness."

Randolph snatched up another little smoked salmon sandwich and asked me if I had ever been to a speakeasy.

"Oh, no, but my brothers have told me about a place they have been. It takes more than an hour to get there by motorcar, and it is in a cave," I replied.

Once more, they looked at me as if I had told them we kept cattle in the house back in Missouri.

Joan pointed an orange scone at me and said, "A cave?"

"It isn't as it sounds. The place has tables with checkered linen and a jazz band. It's like any nightclub, but in a cave rather than a building."

Nicholas came to my aid and said, "How innovative."

I sipped my tea and nodded politely. It was time to let someone else speak. I looked to Ruth and asked, "Were you recently in New York?"

Ruth replied, "Just last autumn." She gave a little pout and said, "I had no idea that the Waldorf Astoria was no longer the place to stay."

Attempting to relocate my social status from farmhand to worldly young woman, I remarked, "Yes, it is rather shabby these days. The Plaza Hotel is the place to stay."

Ruth nodded agreeably as Joan shot me a sour glance and dropped her half-eaten scone on the little china plate in her hand.

I made another attempt to move the role of speaker to someone else. Looking to Phyllis, who neither ate nor drank from the selection before us, I asked, "Did you enjoy your trip to New York?"

The last word I had spoken wasn't even off my tongue when I noticed that everyone's eyes, save Phyllis's, turned all beady. It was as if they had just heard a piece of fine crystal being shattered in the next room.

In an icy voice, Phyllis replied, "The trip was fine."

Thinking I hadn't the wits to realize this was a sensitive topic, Ruth quickly said, "I took Phyllis to the states to see a specialist." As she spoke, I couldn't help but glance at Phyllis's left arm, clenched to her tightly, the hand a small fist. "We did not hear the news that we had hoped."

Nicholas stood from his chair and stepped to the side of his fellow cripple, as he had put it. He patted the woman's shoulder and said, "She's doing much better than before the trip."

Phyllis stared at me; rather, she almost seemed to stare through me, as the others nervously said something very agreeable. Nicholas then redirected the conversation. "Right. Well now, tell us about this novel you are writing. Have you secured an agent yet?"

"Not as of yet, although I do have one in mind. His name is Mr. Harland Orenstein." (This is a little token for you, Mr. Orenstein. You see, it took Mr. Jack a full afternoon of placing telephone calls to a number of important people to find out who represented the leading authors of the genre. You should do better to circulate your name.)

Nicholas nodded and said, "Never heard of the chap. How about your plot, I suppose some poor person is going to get bumped off, is that how they say it?"

"Yes, there will have to be a person with a secret, and then someone with motive to do the dirty deed," Lucy remarked with nervous glee.

Randolph mumbled over a mouthful of his sandwich, "I don't care much for all the suspense."

Joan flashed what looked, for an instant, like ugly fangs at her husband and quipped, "I don't know, some people like a good scandal."

Ruth ignored her older sister-in-law's comment and said, "These whodunits, they rely on stock characters, don't they? Have you selected yours?"

I hoped to say something that would not inspire an awkward retort. "Well, I'm still thinking up my cast of suspicious characters."

Lucy said, with the intent to help me, "You do have that Frenchman character." She looked about the curious faces. "He's unable to return home, since he committed a war crime."

Randolph choked on the last bite of his smoked salmon. At that instant, I realized I should have warned Lucy of the vague talk that after the war, a cloud was cast over him.

Quickly, I commented, "The Frenchman that Lucy mentioned was a railcar attendant. He gave me the idea. Perhaps my book will have a mysterious domestic with a secret."

Nicholas pulled his hand away from the back of Phyllis's chair, very quickly. A strangely bemused grin appeared on the grey woman's face for just a second.

Ruth cleared her throat and opened her brass cigarette case. Nicholas crossed the floor to his wife with his lighter in hand.

Once Ruth had taken a long drag and exhaled the smoke, she said in almost stony pitch, "Speaking of the stock characters, I suspect you'll want to meet the vicar, but of course, he's a bore. His wife has already invited you to luncheon tomorrow; we made the mistake of telling her about your visit. She reads a lot of those books and thinks she knows something about them. I don't know that I can stand it. Phyllis, perhaps you can take the young ladies?"

Phyllis mumbled something agreeable, and I will tell you, the thought of spending an extended amount of time with the woman chilled my blood.

Ruth remained in full control of the conversation—there would be no more mishaps. "And you'll need to go to the pub to see the local country ruffians."

Randolph said rather jovially, "Maybe that sleuthing eye of yours will detect the rascal who hit Nicky."

Forced laughter followed Randolph's remark.

I had no desire for more tea, so I carefully placed my cup and saucer on the low table before me. I noticed the butler make eyes at the serving girl, and an instant later, she swooped in and began collecting the dishes, quite precisely, very quietly. I found myself wishing my notebook was handy; I wanted to record her skilled manner at going unnoticed by everyone but me.

Phyllis had said something, and it took a moment before I realized her comment had been directed at me. "I beg your pardon?"

Sounding like the stern nuns my mother warned me about, she repeated herself, "I said, do you have a plot?"

I gave a little shrug and admitted, "I have several; I must decide on one."

Nicholas remarked, "I just picked up a mystery type book the last time I was in town." He looked to the butler and asked, "What's it called?"

"*Remittance Delayed*, by a gentleman with the last name of Holliston. It is in the library. Shall I collect it?"

"No, thank you, Henderson." Nicholas looked back to me and asked, "Have you read it?" (Now, here, I have named the butler; other than Clarice, I have avoided naming the domestics, as they haven't been important to my story. Lucy read in a journal on writing that an author should limit the number of characters for a reader to remember. Thus, by naming Henderson, it must now surely be recognized that he will become a familiar figure in the rest of my manuscript. Because of the fact that the butler virtually ran the household, it seems difficult to me to leave him unnamed. This is an instance when I believe a seasoned editor will be of help to my work.)

"No, what is it about?" I asked curiously.

"The main character kills his nephew for money, and so far, it seems he's getting away with it."

Lucy put a finger to her lip and said, "How dastardly. Why did the protagonist need money so badly?"

Nicholas replied, "The chap couldn't control his wife's spending...habits..." As his words failed him, everyone looked to Joan, who was leaning toward her husband as he lit her cigarette.

I think my heartbeat doubled.

Phyllis was impervious to the awkwardness. "May I suggest a plot?"

I nodded my chin, vigorously.

"Unrequited love inspires an attempted murder; your sleuth must deduce the criminal before he or she strikes again." With that said, she pointed toward the brass cigarette case on the coffee table.

Nicholas fetched what Phyllis wanted and then lit it. We all watched in silence as she inhaled deeply and then blew out the many whirling tendrils of smoke, enveloping her in a little cloud of grey.

Chapter Four

Dinner, served at seven thirty, went much more smoothly than tea. Each couple had enjoyed a cocktail or two before Lucy and I joined them in evening dress within the black and white Formica-clad dining room.

To my relief, Phyllis did not join us. She sent word by one of the maids that she was tired and had little appetite.

This upset Ruth, but no one else seemed to mind the stark woman's absence; I certainly did not.

There was much talk of horses and golfing, subjects that Lucy was in her element discussing. Once, when my companion remarked that we had the proper attire packed away for some such sport, Joan managed to retort, "Of course you do, Miss Wallace; that outfit was on page fourteen of the catalog."

There was a little jolt, and it would seem that her husband kicked her under the table. Joan drained her glass of wine as if quenching a fire in her throat and then fell silent for a bit.

Nicholas told dull stories about Pearce Manor's lackluster history. This was quite comforting. I felt like a child being lulled to sleep with the retelling of an old Aesop's fable.

After dinner was finished, we went to the library. This room, blessed be, had not been redone in art deco. One wall was a series of windows and French doors leading out to an enclosed garden. Opposite of this, the wall was lined with filled bookshelves, broken only by the double doors leading into the room from the hall. A fantastic marble fireplace was alight, with mirror-faced doors on either side, leading to a room yet unseen.

More drinks were served, and cigarette smoke filled the air. To the obvious relief of Ruth, Phyllis joined us for the remainder of the evening.

She and Ruth partnered for a game of bridge against Joan and Lucy—an odd pairing this seemed to me. Sitting on the oversized leather davenport, pretending to listen to the brothers tell me about the locals, I watched how Phyllis had to place her hand of cards on the table and pull out the card she was tossing to the pile, then she again lifted the cards with her good hand. Always, her left arm remained drawn tightly to her thin body.

I also observed that, though seated at the same table, playing the same game, Phyllis and Joan ignored each other. There was no hostility between the two; they just acted as if the other weren't there.

From time to time, each wife would glance toward her husband, questing for the subject of our trite conversation.

Already half asleep, Lucy and I bade the group goodnight once Joan became too intoxicated to continue playing cards.

Phyllis gave me a cool smile and reminded me, "We'll have luncheon with the vicar's wife tomorrow. Don't stay up all night plotting your murder. Trust me, you will need your rest."

This warning had jolted me awake, and I lay in my bed, unable to sleep. An hour passed, and then another. I decided I might find the book that Nicholas had mentioned earlier and crept down to the library, hoping the family had long since retired for the evening.

A single lamp lit only a corner of the large room. I had thought it left on by mistake until a man's friendly voice said, "May I help you, Mrs. Stayton?"

The butler, Henderson, stood from the couch; a book was in his hand. He was a tall fellow. I suspected him to be fifty years old. The man seemed fit, with only a tinge of grey in his dark hair.

"Oh, I am sorry to disturb you, Henderson. I was just looking for that new mystery that Cousin Nicholas told me about."

"You aren't disturbing me at all," he said kindly. "Yes, let's see." Gently, he placed the book he was reading on the coffee table and then went to a little desk. "Here it is."

I clutched my robe and made several quick strides to prevent the man from having to bring the novel to me. "Thank you."

He smiled, amused by my manners. "You are welcome, Mrs. Stayton. Although, I might say," he lifted his book from the table, "you may find more inspiration in this."

Smiling, I asked, "What are you reading?"

"Edgar Allan Poe. I was just about to finish *The Tell-Tale Heart*. This is a book of his short stories."

"Oh, those are quite clever," I said agreeably.

"Would you prefer this?" Henderson gestured with the book in his hand.

I found so much of Poe's work to be tragically romantic; after all, he too had lost his spouse. "I couldn't; some of his stories are…somewhat dark for me. Back home, when the little budgie talks from his cage, I'm horrified that he might say, *nevermore*."

Henderson did not make that forced, seemingly polite, laugh that I do so hate; he merely smiled.

I glanced at the elegant dog, stretched out and relaxed by the smoldering fire. Henderson took notice and said, "I should have carried him up the stairs an hour ago. I imagine Mrs. Ruth will miss him if she wakes of the night."

"He won't climb the stairs? I never knew of a dog that couldn't make his way from floor to floor."

"Nate's dumbfounded by them; he tried coming down once but almost ended up like Miss Masterson." The butler's face froze in a grimace, and he looked quite ashamed of himself.

"Is that what happened to Phyllis?" I inquired, sounding as ill-mannered as those who asked how my dear Xavier found his way to Heaven.

Henderson nodded his chin, gravely. "She fell from the stairs, yes, two years ago now."

"How awful."

"There was much nerve damage. She could never return to her work."

"What did she do?"

He looked at me, a little surprised by the question. "She was Mrs. Ruth's secretary."

A thought flashed through my mind, *A domestic with a secret.* Nicholas had seemed quite startled when I had made the vague comment.

"Are you all right, Mrs. Stayton?" Henderson asked.

How long had I stared toward nothing? "Oh, yes. I am fine."

"If you won't be needing anything else, I should carry Nate upstairs." He smiled at me, set down Poe's works on the davenport, and then took a step toward the drowsy dog.

I'm not sure why, but I asked in an excited, almost shrill voice, "Tell me, Henderson, why is it that the butler so often *did it*?"

He paused and turned back to me. "Because, ma'am," he began in his fabulously deep British voice, "the domestics move about the house without suspicion. No one would think anything if they saw me coming or going from a room; it is quite expected. I could slip into your bedchamber and replace your headache pills with poison, or leave a pistol in the drawer where you keep your gloves with ease."

"So true," I said.

"May I make a bold statement, Mrs. Stayton?"

"Of course." His insight had been incredibly valuable thus far.

"In such a story, you would make a perfect red herring."

I clapped my hands together. "Why is that?"

"Foreigners are always suspicious."

Smiling, I said, "Am I suspicious, Henderson?"

He bent at his knees and scooped the large dog up into his arms. Then, turning to face me, he said, "Not in the slightest, ma'am."

"Good night, Henderson," I told him, concealing my childish disappointment.

"Good night, Mrs. Stayton."

I held the mystery novel that I had come down to fetch tightly to my chin as I glanced down onto the collection of Poe's work. I thought to myself, *We loved with a love that was more than love.* No, I would never be able to read that's man's sorrowful work again.

Randolph sauntered into the dining room and made a show of sniffing the air. Lucy and I were lifting the lids of the chafing dishes, inspecting the morning's offering. Scrambled eggs, baked ham, bacon, and smoked fish made up the hot portions.

"Little brother is presenting you with a fine English breakfast, I see." He slipped rather close to my side and eyed the ham greedily. "Without guests, we are forced to subside on a bowl of porridge, maybe a piece of moldy fruit, if we are lucky." I wondered if there was something to his little joke.

"Morning, ladies," said Nicholas, entering the room, which was basking in the morning sunlight. I noticed the stiffness in his step, a reminder of his motorcar accident. "Randolph, you are up rather early."

"I smelled bacon and remembered that we had company," Randolph replied sarcastically.

Nicholas gave him a perturbed smile and said, "That's why Nate is at the top of the stairs whining; you two dogs smell fresh meat." He then turned to us and said, "Ladies, do help yourselves. Breakfast is an informal meal in this household. Ruth won't be out of bed for an hour, and only the devil knows when Joan will join the living."

Lucy and I filled our plates and sat side by side at the long dining table. Randolph joined us, and his younger brother, who had just a croissant with a bit of jam before him, glared at Randolph's overflowing dish.

Lucy, aware of the tension, tapped the book beside her plate and said, "Nicholas, how far into this sordid tale are you?"

A natural smile graced the man's face as he turned his attentions to my good-natured friend. "The dastardly deed just happened."

She gave a giggle and told him she'd started reading the story just after dawn, when she found it at my dressing table.

"What do you think so far?" asked Nicholas.

"It is unique. I am waiting for the clever detective to arrive," she replied and gave the tome a thump with her knuckles.

With a mouthful of bacon, Randolph remarked, "I just don't like mysteries. I feel something of an idiot when I can't figure them out."

"What type of book do you enjoy?" I asked in an effort to be friendly.

"Yes, Randolph, what type of book do you enjoy?" Nicholas echoed.

"Give me an adventure, some classic that is beloved by the ages," Randolph replied to me, ignoring his brother.

"Robin Hood, perhaps? Stealing from the rich and giving to the poor," said Lucy, all too innocently.

Nicholas and Randolph remained silent, and the same pained expression crossed their similar faces.

Joan glided into the room just on cue, and having heard Lucy, she retorted, "Dear child, maybe that's what your companion's side of the Stayton family does, but not us."

The brothers shared a mirthless laugh, and then Randolph asked, "Aren't you awake rather early?"

She barked out for a hovering little maid to fetch her a cup that had been run under scalding hot water before replying to her husband, "That damned dog was whining at the top of the staircase."

Nicholas pushed back from the table, ready to solve the problem. Joan stopped him. "Be still, Nicky. I gave Henderson the what for about it already."

The ill-tempered woman sat across from me. She stared down the maid who returned with her coffee cup, held by a napkin.

Joan, as I have said before, was very attractive. As it would seem, though, the combination of early morning and a hangover, did not suit her. Dark circles gave age to the woman's face. Fine lines about her eyes spoke of a tension and unhappiness that I hoped never to know.

She poured coffee from the silver decanter on the table and carefully tapped the handle of the cup to see how hot it was. She reached back and grimaced before looking up and catching my eye.

Joan remarked, "I must look a fright, don't I?"

"Not at all. I was taking note of how you have your cup heated before you fill it. The habit might make an interesting detail in my book."

She gave me a curt nodded and said in a mocking tone, *"The exacting actions of a finicky woman caught my inquisitive eye."*

Randolph spoke over his last bite of scrambled eggs, "Better than, '*The gaiety of intoxication was replaced with the sorrow of sobriety.'*"

Lucy's toe tapped my ankle, and I knew what she was thinking. If only she'd brought her little notepad down to record the banter.

I reached over to pick up *Remittance Delayed,* and then cheerfully said, "I don't think that type of talk will be found in this book; it's a different sort of mystery."

Nicholas matched my tone, and thankful for the distraction, he asked, "Do you not like it?"

"I wouldn't say that, but it doesn't speak to my muse," I replied.

"I plan on reading it from cover to cover and then breaking down the flow of action. There is a formula to all of these novels, you know," Lucy said, pitching in with her usual sunshiny disposition. (I make note here that I fear Lucy is not given adequate depth in this manuscript. As it is she who has typed it from my notes, I think she has subtracted much of her character to fit the expected nature of the *sidekick*. Just this, via stern dictation, was added in hopes that the prospective editor can help to make Lucy shine as she should.)

Ruth joined us before anything else might be said. Nate was at her side as she walked toward the sideboard. "Good morning," she said to the ensemble.

Nicholas stood and asked, "Did the dog wake you, my dear?"

Ruth removed the lid from one of the chafing dishes and then handed the Afghan hound a sliver of bacon. "Of course not," she replied as she put together a small plate of food.

Ruth's presence seemed to still everyone. Conversation was very mundane, blessedly so, I might add. They spoke of the dryness of the weather, the anticipation of a county festival, and the gossip of locals I would never meet.

I thought to myself, *This is background dialogue, the type of things said that gives insight to the day-to-day of the characters, which will make them feel real.*

The plates were cleared, another scalding hot cup was fetched for Joan, and then the brothers excused themselves.

Ruth made an attempt to advise me on my novel, but admitted that mysteries confounded her. She preferred to read the last few pages of the book first, and then lost interest some place halfway through the story.

Lucy and I told our hostess and her silent sister-in-law that we were going to sit out in the garden and discuss my latest ideas.

Ruth said something agreeable and then added, "I don't think I shall join you for luncheon. I'll have a call placed with my excuse. I can't see that innocent face of yours turning a lie, so if the vicar's wife comments on my headache, let Phyllis make the response."

Lucy and I both penciled a number of observations and thoughts into our notebooks. Miss X hadn't yet a crime to solve, but she did have a number of clues. The dog that couldn't manage stairs, the piping hot piece of china, and a deceitful message to the vicar's wife—these points of interest were rife with suspicion.

As the morning went on, Lucy hinted that she preferred to stay at Pearce Manor and riffle through the pages of *Remittance Delayed*.

The thought of riding alone in the car with Phyllis did not thrill me, but I suspected that sweet Lucy feared the ashen woman more than I did.

After changing into something suitable for luncheon, I found Phyllis waiting for me in the foyer. Her short black hair gleamed in the sunlight pouring through the open doors. She wore a dark jacket with matching skirt, and a ruffled grey shirt hung loosely from her gaunt frame; it seemed to lean against the buttoned jacket for support.

"What do you say, Mrs. Stayton, let's get this over with," she said with dry humor.

I thought it odd that the driver did not assist Phyllis into the car. I was too unfamiliar with the woman to suggest my aid. Once she was settled, I climbed inside. Only after we were moving did she speak. "You aren't what I had pictured."

"No?" I replied, somewhat fearful of her explanation.

She shook her lean face. "No, I thought you would have a painted face, wear those stringy flapper dresses, and say annoying things like, *the cat's meow,* or some such talk."

I felt myself shrink a little. "I hadn't realized that I'd made such a bad impression on the Staytons."

"Oh, no, I conjured the image of a Ziegfeld girl. Nicholas and Ruth commented after the wedding that you were very sweet. That was really all they said about you. Mostly, they complained about your mother-in-law, but, of course, you know how they dislike her."

I wasn't sure how to respond to either statement that Phyllis had made. A rebuttal was unnecessary, as she asked, "You don't smoke, do you, child?"

"No, I never got the knack for it. Xavier gave me a lovely cigarette holder. I use it from time to time at parties, but I just puff them," I said, sounding very young, very foolish, and I'm sure, very nervous.

"They're awful things; keep to those cloves I see you sneaking onto your tongue," she said slyly as she fished her cigarette case from her purse.

I smiled, and tried to remember when she had witnessed this habit of mine. Rarely did I chew on a clove unless melancholy or perturbed.

After a moment of silence, Phyllis asked, "Why do you chew on them? Do they taste good?"

I could have ended the inquiry by agreeing with the woman's suggestion. However, there was something about Phyllis that told me she would recognize a lie.

"My husband chewed them; it was how his governess broke him of biting his nails. He never gave them up." I reached into my handbag and pulled out a little silver monogrammed snuffbox that had belonged to him to show the woman. "The taste is both sweet and spicy and was always on his breath. When I chew one, it reminds me of his kiss."

Phyllis reached out with her good hand and patted my arm. This action surprised me.

Blushing from sharing something so intimate, I said, "I beg your pardon, I shouldn't have said—"

"Now, don't be a silly fool with me like you are with the Staytons." She paused, and a genuine smile cracked her ridged exterior. "He was a very fortunate young man to have found such a love in his short life."

I wasn't sure what to say.

"Despite your misfortune, you are a happy girl, as you should be. There is nothing wrong with that. Don't think the air at Pearce Manor is normal—it isn't."

I gave her a nervous smile and glanced to see that the little window between us and the driver was closed. Phyllis noticed this and said, "Oh, let him be damned for what he thinks. Now, light my cigarette."

The vicar's wife was, in fact, an absolute bore. A small woman with nervous fingers and darting eyes, she looked like a librarian just itching to shush someone. She served a strange medley of what might have been two evenings worth of leftovers. My American tongue had taken well enough to the food in London, but the country cuisine offered to me went down rather slowly.

From the get-go, she told me she understood that I was collecting information for a whodunit. Proudly, she pointed at stack of books, and named authors such as Emilie Gaboriau, Sir Arthur Conan Doyle, and Charles Dickens among her favorites.

Phyllis reached for the woman's copy of *Great Expectations* and said, "I'll give you there's some mystery to this one, but I dare say it isn't a whodunit."

Our host seemed uncomfortable with Phyllis. "Do you like that book, Miss Masterson?" she asked, rather cautiously.

"I find some of the passages speak to me," Phyllis said, and then she quoted, *"In a word, I was too cowardly to do what I knew was right, as I had been too cowardly to avoid doing what I knew to be wrong."*

Not sure what to make of Phyllis's comment, the vicar's wife invited us inside her cramped dining room, and we suffered through her meal. (The woman did provide me with many interesting facts about the locals, kindly omitting their names, of course. For the sake of pacing, I shall jump over all this; it seems after nearly fifty pages typed, we haven't a crime, victim, or suspects. Lucy reminds me it is preferred that the murder takes place earlier in the manuscript, so I will be agreeable to the insight of an editor to make alterations. That being stated, I'm not fond of the stories where you come in at the murder and then digress back to what leads up to the crime.)

Running out of gossip, our hostess offered us what she called freshly baked pie. Phyllis rose from the table and said, "I will pass. I need a cigarette." She held out her good arm and waved at the vicar's wife. "Yes, I know that you are allergic. I'll go out to the garden."

"Asthma and all," the little woman told me. I could not help but notice that her spirits lightened once Phyllis was away.

I had just stuck my fork into the piece of pie that had been served to me already cut and on a plate, not sliced from a warm pan for me to see, when my hostess's voice dropped to the tone of a conspirator. "You know, I do so hate to ask, but these past few years it has been such a mystery as to what happened to young Master Stayton, might you tell me?"

I made the smug smile shared by conspirators and replied, "The family doesn't like to discuss the topic; I gather, as the vicar's wife, you can keep this just between us?"

"Of course, child, but of course I can." She was nearly drowning in ecstasy; the thought of sharing such a secret was like gold to this woman, who traded in gossip.

"I'm sure you knew this already, but my dear Xavier was an explorer," I began.

Her little head bobbed up and down. "Oh, yes, child."

"Well, he went to Italy to see Pompeii, that city in ruins."

"I've heard of it, a debauched place, they say," she said nearly in a whisper.

"Indeed; so he went sightseeing in the city, and he was enraptured by its beauty. He wanted to see the place from a vantage point, so he hiked up to the top of Mt. Vesuvius," I told the woman.

Her dull little eyes were kindled with dark curiosity.

"He made it to the summit, and then, gazing down at the majestic ruins...he took a step back." I paused for effect, then dabbed my cheek with a handkerchief. "And by the most horrible of accidents, my dearest love tumbled into the volcano."

The vicar's wife let out a little yelp and shoved a white knuckle between her yellowed teeth.

I glanced into the shadow of the nearby doorway and saw that Phyllis was watching me; an amused smile graced her skull-like face.

The car was bowling down the lane at full speed when Phyllis asked me to light another cigarette for her. She took a long drag and said, "Might I ask you a question? You know I'm not like Ruth; I'm very frank, and you can so no."

I knew the woman's question. I didn't mind answering her. "I don't mind."

"Why did you lie to the vicar's wife about your husband's death?"

She was too sophisticated to pry into my business any further, so I felt at ease to respond honestly, "My husband had intended on becoming an explorer; he wanted to travel the world. Instead, he met me and cut his journey short.

"His death was not becoming of his character. When people ask me such a horrible question, such a personal question, they deserve the far-fetched answers I give them."

Phyllis nodded and replied, "I respect that." She paused and put her cigarette to her lips. She made some attempt to blow the smoke she exhaled towards the partially open window before saying, "Few people receive the death they deserve."

I became the people I despised and asked, "Tell me, Miss Masterson, how would you die?"

For an instant, I saw past her near-constant grimace and the coldness that enveloped her soul, as she smiled and said, "How did Julius Caesar put it: *swiftly and without warning.*"

I refused to make that mirthless laugh that people are so comforted by. Instead, I told her, "If only we each had a glass of champagne to toast your wit."

Phyllis reached out and grasped my elbow with her good hand, and earnestly, she told me, "Child, I do like you."

This was a personal triumph. I said nothing more, and we rode on in contented silence.

Chapter Five

Henderson opened the car door and assisted Phyllis. As I climbed out of the car, the butler told the driver, "Go back into town. Mrs. Stayton and Miss Wallace should be done with their shopping soon."

Curious, I asked, "Lucy went to town with Ruth?"

Phyllis said something in parting and returned to the house. Henderson explained that after taking me and Miss Masterson to luncheon, the driver returned so that Ruth could make a quick trip into town. Lucy had gone with Ruth so she might purchase a thesaurus.

I felt a little lost without my companion. Returning to my room, a blanket of quiet hushed the large home. Standing at the mantel, I looked upon my photographs of Xavier and no longer felt alone.

"He was such a handsome young man." Joan's hard-edged voice was unexpected. She had slipped in through the partially open doorway.

Startled, I turned to see her gliding toward me. Taking a deep breath, my heart rate slowed, and I replied, "Yes."

Joan stepped beside me; she was turned out in riding gear and smelled of the outdoors. The woman picked up a photograph of my husband in his golf attire. "He cut a dashing figure, didn't he?"

I repeated my simple answer, "Yes."

She placed the photograph back among the rest and said, "He was quite the sportsman."

This was a misconception. Xavier was very handsome, and his physique spoke of his attempts at all manner of sport, thus his photographs when in the costume of athletics were very impressive. The truth was different. He injured himself and others more often than he succeeded at the point of the competition. He could scarcely walk straight down a sidewalk, let alone hit a small white ball onto a green, or keep his tennis racket from becoming entangled in the net.

I said something agreeable to Joan. She looked me over and asked, "You survived the vicar's wife?"

"She was easy enough; her cooking seemed the more obvious hazard." This was mean-spirited of me, but I thought Joan might become more agreeable with me if I spoke in her vernacular.

Joan barked her ugly laugh. She leaned into me, twisted her head over her shoulder to glance at the door, and then said, slyly, "You managed well enough with Phyllis, I see."

"Oh, yes."

"Don't trust her. She's a snake in the grass. I'd keep your door locked too. Several years ago, I found her sneaking about our room. My perfume was always missing, and my lipstick was mashed about the tube. She acts disinterested, cool as a cucumber, but she's rather meddlesome."

I just nodded, unsure what to say.

"I hear your mouse of a friend ran off on you. Fancy a trip to the pub? Get a chance to see some of the locals waste their Tuesday afternoon?"

I didn't really want to go off on an expedition with Joan; I doubted that I had the calluses to survive her.

"That does sound rather a fun thing, but the car went off to pick up Ruth and Lucy."

"No matter, we have more cars!" she said sarcastically.

Slipping through the French doors of the library, Joan led me to the little car park beside a long carriage house. A dark red automobile glistened in the late afternoon sunshine.

"It's a two-seater," I remarked, concerned.

"It's an Amilcar, French, quite fast," she told me as she ran a gloved finger on the radiator cap that was fashioned to look like Pegasus.

Small, with a spare tire mounted to the front of the body just between the drive and the front tire, the thing looked rather dangerous.

"Get in," Joan ordered me.

"You drive?" I asked, as I followed her command.

"Of course! You don't?" she said, very pleased with herself.

"No, we've always relied on the driver." I tried to picture my father making his way to the hospital operating his own dark blue Packard. Father was always preoccupied, with what I never knew.

Joan scoffed and said, "I don't see Viviane being the motoring sort, but you should take it up; it's a ripping good time!" and with that said, she gave the gear shift a jerk and pushed the gas pedal to the floor.

Joan drove like a madwoman. I had to pull my hat tight to my head or it would have whipped out of the topless flash of red metal screeching over the ribbon of black road.

She pointed at the gas pedal, the clutch, and the gear shifter, and kept repeating, "It's all really easy," after explaining how each item functioned.

Approaching town, we passed Ruth and Lucy coming from the opposite direction. Lucy and I waved at each other, and I dare say we shared the same pinched smile.

We abandoned the Amilcar in a car park, and with wobbly legs, I followed Joan just down the street to the public house.

She pushed open the door and said, "Here we are."

From the bright light of day, we crossed over to a shadowy den. Smoke hung in the air, clinging to the smell of spilled beer.

A dumpy man leaned against a counter, preaching to a few parishioners. He eyed us suspiciously and then bellowed out, "Mrs. Joan, is that you?"

She called out that it was her, and then asked me what I wanted to drink.

"A glass of sherry would be nice."

She called back to the tavern keeper an order of two pale ales, and then, to me, she said, "You don't have to be all prim and proper with me."

The two beers were delivered to our table, and the proprietor remarked, "We certainly miss seeing you around here."

She cast me an awkward glance and said, "As they say, it has been a dry spring."

The man gave a little laugh and teetered back to those sitting belly to the bar. Joan looked the three men and two women over.

"Not much of interest about them." She leaned very close to my ear. "The little shrew with a scab for a face, she had an abortion."

I almost spit out my mouthful of tangy beer.

Joan's speech was quite slurred before she ran out of gossip about the uninteresting company, who had long ago realized that she was discussing them.

When I suggested we depart, she demanded another drink. I paid the bill with the delivery of what would be her final *one more.*

As she drained the last of the swill, Joan looked into my eyes and said, "I envy you."

This I knew; she was greedy, and I was well provided for. She was also at that age when beautiful women become fearful of their good looks, and I was just blossoming, no longer a girl but a young woman.

What response might I make? All I could do was arch my brow and stare back at her.

"I wish my Randolph had died in the war, and then it would be me who was the pitied widow."

This was not the mean-spirited comment that I had anticipated. I rather wished to reach out and slap her. I would have traded all of the Stayton family fortune, and every moment of my youth, to have Xavier alive and well.

Finally taking charge, I stood and barked out in imitation of Joan's voice, "It is well past time that we leave."

It was a rough start, but I got the French motorcar off and moving. As the thing jerked and hiccupped, Joan laughed wildly.

Once on the country road leading back to Pearce Manor, the intoxicated woman belched before telling me, "You should get your own automobile."

I ignored her, as she deserved to be ignored. The fact was, I had my own car, or rather, I still had Xavier's. It was a handsome German roadster. From time to time, Mr. Jack would take it from the garage and drive me about in it.

Not sure which of the three gears was the correct one to use as I slowed the automobile down, we coasted along the flat driveway to the car park before the carriage house.

The chauffeur was washing the sedan and appeared surprised to see me behind the wheel.

Joan stumbled out of the car as the chauffeur responded to my plea that he deal with the smaller vehicle, which I abandoned, still idling.

Completely oblivious to my anger, Joan remarked, "You did a jolly good job getting us back."

Making no effort to be polite, I snapped at her, "I'm just happy I didn't run someone down."

Joan took a misstep and attempted to focus her red eyes upon me. Nearly stuttering, she responded, "Yes, quite so."

Lucy tapped at my closed bedroom door and called my name. I told her to come in, before placing a clove on my tongue and taking a quick look at Xavier's photos.

"My eyes nearly leapt from my head when I looked out the window and saw you driving…" She saw the expression on my face and fell silent.

"A Christian woman shouldn't know the word that I think that woman is," I admitted.

"Joan? Why, what did she do?" Lucy asked.

"She drank herself stupid." I would not repeat what she said about Randolph. I softened my pitch and said, "I was surprised that Ruth went into town."

Lucy's eyes opened wide. "So was I, except it was all planned out. Before Joan went off to the stables, I heard something said like, 'Best to do it now, while

Phyllis is out of pocket for a change.' I'm just not sure what the *it* was?"

"Where did she go?"

"An alteration lady. Henderson placed a dress box in the trunk in the back of the car. I was dropped off at the book seller's, and Ruth said she'd only be a few minutes," Lucy said, thrilled with the scant bit of mystery.

"Did you see the dress?" I asked.

"No, nor was it brought in from the motorcar when we returned. I think she had a fitting and left the dress with the seamstress."

I repeated what Lucy had heard, "While Phyllis was out of pocket."

Shortly after this discussion, a little pinch-faced maid rapped at my door and said that we were welcome to take tea when we pleased, and that we would be alone. The rest of the family was, as she put it, occupied.

Crossing through the foyer, Henderson called to me and said, "Mrs. Stayton, I directed that the tea be placed in the library rather than the drawing room; this seemed more in keeping with the mood you desire."

Lucy and I nibbled at the little sandwiches and made many notes in our journals. She asked me, "Do you have some phrase that Miss X will be known for?"

"The only thing that comes to mind is, 'I rather think that I've stepped in it.'"

Lucy clapped her hands together and giggled her sweet English laughter.

An instant later, Phyllis slinked into the room, smoke trailing behind her. "Well, that explains the laughter; you two are all alone."

I wouldn't attempt to make excuses for the people she knew all too well. "We are stitching together my plot. I have given some thought to your suggestion of a hopeful lover turned murderer."

Phyllis said, "Why must they be a murderer? Why not let them fail at the crime? Then your sleuth can catch them on their second attempt—quite the heroine she would be."

Lucy poured a cup of tea for Phyllis and said, "Oh, how clever."

"Yes, I do like the idea." I looked into Phyllis's pleased eyes after she had sat down near me. "You really don't mind that I use your suggestion?"

She sipped from her cup and told me, "I shall consider it my gift to the world of literature."

Phyllis went on and made several more splendid suggestions. Lucy and I took detailed notes.

Dinner was, I should say, strained. Joan was absent. Randolph remarked that she had a headache from being outdoors for too much of the day, and there was a mumble of assent from Ruth.

Phyllis sent word that she'd eaten too much at tea and would skip dinner. This seemed odd because I didn't recall seeing her eat a single scone or deviled egg. She had just sipped her tea and smoked cigarette after cigarette while she kindled the fire of my literary imagination.

I had wanted to ask her if there had ever been a man she'd loved so much she thought of ending his life had he refused to fall to Cupid's arrow. Of course, I held my tongue.

As the dinner conversation remained somewhat placid, I thought to myself that perhaps they'd made an arrangement among themselves to be agreeable and suffer through the next few days of my stay without the constant bickering.

If so, Joan's absences would make an easy start. Randolph would need to watch his quips, while Nicholas and Ruth were both capable of being ever so charming when they chose.

The courses were served, all very nice, and then we made our way to the drawing room. There was talk of playing cards when Phyllis joined us, looking rather tired from the long day. However, we never opened a deck.

Instead, Ruth told me and Lucy all that she knew about French art. She was fond of the safe subject. I wished I had my pencil and pad, but I could tell from Lucy's occasional question that she was recording all of the information in her head.

Once Ruth had tired of the subject of French art, Randolph, who had been on his best behavior, asked, "How was the luncheon with the vicar's wife?"

"Tedious," responded Phyllis before I could. She then leaned forward so that Nicholas could light another cigarette for her.

"She did enjoy entertaining us," I added.

"Did she tell you all about the many mystery books she has read?" Ruth inquired, sipping very slowly on a snifter of brandy.

"Yes, and some of the local scandal as well," I replied.

I could not help but notice Phyllis and Nicholas's eyes meet for just an instant.

"She keeps spreading lies about a poor wretch who lost her child. I hope you know she can't be believed," Ruth said. She hadn't noticed the look passed between her husband and her former secretary.

Phyllis let out a puff of smoke from her dark-stained lips, and added, "Or trusted."

Nate stood from the floor at Ruth's side; the dog walked around in a tight circle and then lay back down at his mistress's feet. She reached down and stroked him before casting a queer gaze at Phyllis.

Randolph, now inspecting his nails, asked me, "It is the end of day two, master sleuth, have you your clues, suspects, and a villain?"

I looked quickly across the room at the faces that watched me and replied, "I do."

Phyllis, very dramatically, flicked her ash into a silver dish and said, "Now you just need a victim."

Ruth, her husband, and his brother made the polite laughter that was called for by such a sarcastically said statement, while the domestics observed our strangely tense moment in silence.

Chapter Six

Lucy and I ate breakfast alone. Both Nicholas and Randolph passed through the dining room and gave their greetings, but neither joined us. Once more, we were warned that their wives slept in, and we shouldn't expect to see them until luncheon. This suited us just fine.

Lucy and I set up in the library, and I dictated the outline of my whodunit. The story went as follows, Miss X, with her trusty sidekick, Miss W, were invited to a country estate for the weekend. Miss W's uncle was hosting a celebration, as he planned to announce his engagement to the Lady A.

Near tragedy strikes when a storm knocks down the power lines. Gathered in the drawing room, so that Uncle can share the good news, the guests find themselves in darkness and hear a terrible thud.

The light comes back on, and poor Uncle has been struck on the back of the head by a candelabra. It is now up to Miss X, with the help of Miss W, to first deduce the motivation, and then the culprit.

As with so many other novels of the genre, I needed to come up with a character who was a major or a colonel. I would have to study on the Great War to give him a credible background.

I had my vicar's wife, and knew the actual woman would be ever so flattered once she read my work. (This does remind me, I will be in need of at least two dozen advanced copies once this goes into publication. I shall leave these arrangements to you. Mr. Jack can see to having them parceled after I have made some personalized inscription in each.)

The idea of the poor local woman, who either had an abortion or a miscarriage, at first, fit my role as the lady suffering from unrequited love. However, had my intended victim actually had a dalliance with the unfortunate female, then he would seem less sympathetic.

The thought also passed my mind that my mother would be reading my novel, and I didn't know what she or Mother Stayton would think of my inclusion of the topic.

Over the next few days, Lucy and I toiled tirelessly. My hosts, realizing we no longer required much entertaining, left us to our work. A few neighbors and friends dropped in to visit from time to time, and we met them cordially. Ruth would give us their story before their arrival and suggest who might fit well into my mystery.

Tea would be served, and they would speak to me politely until my novelty wore off and conversation would drift back to the local topics of interest.

Otherwise, we met the family only for dinner, where they would question me on Miss X's pursuits. I was childishly vague, assuring them that once the story was complete, I would, as it were, make a full confession.

Phyllis was the only person permitted to look at the progress. She would carefully grasp a lit cigarette in her injured hand, clasped below her bosom, and flip through the typed pages with her good hand.

Of points of style, she gave no mention. As to the happenings of the story, she made insightful suggestions. Since I had the intention of dedicating the work to my dearest Xavier, I would need to give Phyllis endless praise, just after Lucy, in my author's notes. (Lucy has commented that the comma key on this brand-new typewriter seems to be showing wear rather quickly. If this is but a hint on her part that my sentence structure should be altered, I leave this to the editor.)

With our intended departure set for the coming Monday morning, we worked late into the night and rose early of the morning to finish the first draft by Friday afternoon.

At dinner that evening, I wore my most elegant emerald green satin gown. Pearls clung to my neck, and I dabbed as much powder on my face as I dared. Lucy was dressed to the nines as well; she looked ever so smart.

In my honor, several of the well-placed locals whom we had met over the week were invited to supper. I was both delighted and ashamed that the dominating topic of conversation was my whodunit.

The guests were all charming and so inquisitive. I did not feel as much the out-of-place American as I did the fascinating author.

By request, I described several of my characters. There was the spurned lover; she was a mysterious woman with fiery red hair, which matched her bad humor. Next, the devoted fiancée, quiet in voice, but ever so jealous. The uncle, good-natured at heart, and being driven mad by the secret he has kept from his fiancée. Lastly, was the estranged husband of the spurned lover, who wants her back, only to save face.

The dinner guests all mumbled words of excitement and congratulations to me. However, Joan, Ruth, Nicholas, and Randolph all stared at me with cold eyes and clenched jaws.

After the last course of the wonderful meal had been served, and I had been toasted by those gathered, it was suggested that the menfolk adjourn to the stately library, while the ladies made their way to the art deco drawing room.

Several of the women made a fuss over the Afghan hound. Nate languished beside Ruth's feet, unsure of the many guests.

At this moment that I was not the center of attention, I remembered what I had packed away in my room.

My auburn hair was done up so nice, my pearl earrings and choker necklace had received so much notice, I just wanted to add to my brief dalliance with sophistication. I slipped away while cocktails were still being served, intent to nab from my jewelry box the cigarette holder Xavier had given me.

How fashionable I thought I would appear. *So worldly, this young lady from the continent was,* they might think.

Bless the Almighty, my high heels and long gown kept me from bounding up the staircase, forgetting what little actual dignity I possessed.

I came to my room and noticed the door was ajar. I froze, unsure if a servant was merely preparing my bed, or if someone who should not have been was in my room.

A confrontation was undesirable. My ruby ring was on my finger, and Xavier's snuffbox was inside the little purse I clasped. These were the two most important things in the world to me, and no cat burglar would care to make off with the many photos of my beloved, so I decided to quietly turn back and find Henderson. He could deal with the unknown intruder.

This was not to be; my back now to the doorway, I was startled to hear my name spoken. I turned back to see Nicholas, his complexion drained of color. He was the last person I had expected to be sneaking about my room. What does one say to their host at such an occasion?

"Cousin Nicky," I said. This choice of words sounded very odd from me, as I had never been invited to call him Nicky. "What a startle you've given me. I was just coming up to get something and realized that it was in my clutch." Concluding my lie, I flashed him my little black purse; doing so, I saw how plain it appeared, ill-fitting alongside my satin gown that had looked so sleek, so sharp on the mannequin at H and N.

Nicholas appreciated the lie and replied in form. "I had to run up here for a moment, and I noticed your door was ajar. I stepped in to make sure Nate hadn't nosed his way inside."

No longer surprised, I was now suspicious. There was no need to mention that the dog was in the drawing room with his wife, or that the helpless creature could not manage stairs and would have had to have been carried to the second floor.

We smiled at each other, and we both saw past the forced expressions. After a moment of awkward silence, Nicholas gestured toward the stairs.

I recalled his reaction to my comment, *a domestic with a secret,* and the way he had jerked away from

Phyllis. Could he be capable of pushing a woman down a flight of stairs?

I would not take the chance. I made a little pout and tapped my clutch again, "On second thought," I said, "I'm not sure that I do have it."

I stepped past him and pushed the door wide open. He gave me a nervous smile and suggested that his guests would be missing him. I agreed and shut the door firmly after he took a single step back.

There was no mistake about what had just happened. I flipped the lock, without waiting politely for him to be far enough away that the action would go unnoticed. Quite the contrary, I wanted Cousin Nicky to know that I was on to him.

Looking about the room, nothing seemed disturbed. Stepping over to my writing desk, I inspected my manuscript. As anticipated, the domed glass paperweight had been moved. I had set the object directly over the working title of my story, in a way so that the *X* of *Miss X and the Case of Cupid's Misdeed* created the optical illusion that the letter was three times its actual size. Nicholas had not noticed this detail, and the item was left squarely in the center of the first typed page.

Completely forgetting about my cigarette holder, I returned downstairs to the drawing room. Lucy was at my side in an instant. Handing me a mixed drink, she remarked playfully, "I was about to send Holmes out to look for you."

I didn't want to concern her. I forced a pleased smile and sipped at the rather strong concoction of liquor, named after a line in a jazz song.

The women, all familiar with each other, had broken into three different groups and lounged about the modern room. They cast pleasant smiles on me, but my moment in the spotlight was over. Local gossip, the need for rain, *background dialogue,* this claimed the night from me.

Ruth and Joan separately held court over several women each. Another lady gnawed away at Phyllis, until the gaunt figure gave the wordy woman a pat on the elbow and stalked off to where Lucy and I stood.

She clinked her glass to Lucy's and then mine and said, "You had them all rather captivated."

I had little choice if I was to spare Lucy, at least for the moment, undue concern. I downed my drink and handed the ice-filled glass to my sweet friend. "That was divine. Would you be a dove and get me another?"

Wide-eyed, Lucy inspected the piece of crystal as she took it from me and then went back to the maid stationed at the liquor cabinet.

"Captivated is one word for it. Did you see the look on *their* faces? I caught Nicholas leaving my room just a moment ago; he had taken a look at my manuscript," I told her quickly, as the heat of the drink made its way to my stomach, and the soul of the drink made its way to my head.

"A racy story, all concocted under their roof. Child, they have every reason to wonder about just what you've written and how it will reflect on Pearce Manor," Phyllis replied rather jovially, enjoying her own cocktail.

"The characters have nothing to do with them," I retorted.

Her lips curled, but did not part; there was something sinister about her grin. A second passed, and as Lucy returned, handing me a glass twice the size of the one she'd taken from me, Phyllis

79

suggested, "They are curious. I have a suggestion. Put their minds to ease; share the story with them."

Lucy, whose fear of Phyllis had abated, suggested, "Miss Masterson, you have such a lovely voice; you sound so smart. I think you should do a reading of the manuscript."

Those so very dark eyes of the ashen woman sparkled as she tipped her drink, with her good hand, in my direction and said, "I have a much better idea. Tomorrow evening, after dinner, highlights from *The Case of Cupid's Misdeed* should be acted out."

We all stood in the foyer. After ushering the last guests out the door, Phyllis had put me on the spot and said I had a marvelous suggestion. I mumbled what had been, in fact, her suggestion to our hosts.

"Act it out?" Ruth repeated my words, in a flat, concerned voice.

Phyllis spoke before I could reply. "Well, we are all curious to hear what the dear child has composed this past week. Lucy can't type several copies of it before they depart Monday morning. Assemble the maids and the gardener, whoever else is needed, after dinner tomorrow, and they can act it out for us to watch. They'll just need a little time in the afternoon to learn their bits."

I was no longer sure if Phyllis was out to help me or ruin me. I just smiled and nodded.

"I would enjoy it; wouldn't everyone else?" Phyllis concluded as all others stared at her in disbelief.

Nicholas rubbed his face with his hands and made a grunting noise that seemed to favor the performance. His older brother shrugged and looked to his wife, who stared into her half-empty glass. Back to Ruth, the question was answered, "How nice; we will have a little theatrics, then."

We scattered in different directions of the house while Henderson carried the dog upstairs.

Chapter Seven

After a quick breakfast, Lucy and I worked feverishly on selecting just the right excerpts from my manuscript to be reworked into a script. There was not time to act out the entire plot. Instead, we would witness the attempted murder and the deduction made by Miss X.

Lucy typed out individual sheets of dialogue for our cast. There was no time to correct typos. I penciled in notes that might help direct the characters' actions.

Once a solitary luncheon was served to us, we made ready to gather the cast. It was Phyllis who offered to direct the staff into the library so that we could assign their roles.

Henderson was, of course, cast as *the butler.* The chauffeur was selected to portray the estranged husband; his indifference was perfect to the character. The gardener was given the part of *Uncle,* and seemed thrilled to play the leading role. Two pouting maids were assigned the parts of the culprit and the red herring. The cook and her assistant would stand about and act as the invited quests. Nate was selected to portray the *family cat*; as felines rarely do what they are told, the dog's performance was masterful.

The rehearsal ended when Henderson started to become agitated, and I realized it was getting well on to four o'clock. I dismissed the staff so that they might rush to the kitchen and prepare for tea.

Phyllis had been very quiet as I instructed my actors on their movements. Once Lucy and I were the only ones remaining with her, the woman lounged awkwardly in a high-backed leather chair.

"Bring me a cigarette," she said to whichever of us might comply.

Lucy rushed to follow the command, and then asked, "What did you think?"

"I can think of no actress on the silver screen who might need to worry herself, but that man who plays a tramp might give pause if he realized just anyone can act like a bumbling fool," Phyllis remarked. She sounded rather weary. After a long drag from her cigarette, a glimmer of life came back to her. "All things considered, it was positively entertaining."

I felt rather apprehensive and said, "This might be a mistake."

Lucy misunderstood my concern and said, "Oh no, it will come off."

Extending her good hand, as tendrils of smoke rose from the burning object past her fingertips, Phyllis pointed at the candelabra. "For the performance this evening, switch that with a candlestick. I believe the candelabra would actually do someone in."

I was too nervous to join the others for tea, if in fact they even bothered to make their way into the gay drawing room where the little feast would be laid out.

I told Lucy that I needed to take a little rest. She thought this was a good idea and left me alone to contemplate. The span of two hours passed all too quickly as I reconsidered becoming a famous painter.

Satin after seven, as Randolph had said. I combed my auburn hair away from my face and tucked it behind my ears. Donning my most modest pieces of jewelry, I slipped into a dark blue gown. The elegant thing looked like something Joan would wear, and I considered changing.

There was a rap at my door, and I knew what I wore would be of little concern for the four people waiting to see my little story acted out.

Phyllis greeted me outside of my room. Her dark purple velvet gown was a contrast to her typical grey or black ensembles. She took a long, appraising look at me and said, "Lovely."

Smiling, I reached to close my door and then halted, "I forgot to spritz myself with perfume."

Phyllis stopped me. "Don't worry with it. I detest perfume." She bade me to interlock elbows with her, the good one, and we glided down the stairs, ever so gracefully.

It seemed that she had determined to give me strength through this event that she'd put me up to.

Dinner was filled with tedious small talk, the kind of stuff a reader would skim through, stopping only at a name or a well-turned phrase.

While Ruth and Nicholas's wineglasses were often refilled, Randolph shot his wife several stern glances that seemed to slow down her intake.

The staff was clumsy and preoccupied. Were they saying their lines over and over in their heads, or cursing me for making my intrepid journey to Pearce Manor?

Sentences trailed off, polite guffaws were brief, small helpings of tasteless food were moved from one side of a dish to another, until dessert was served in near silence.

Several times, I thought about giving a great laugh, and then announcing, *On second thought, I don't think my muse is a writer after all. Let's forget about acting out my attempt, and just play bridge after dinner. When I return to London, I think I'll have Mr. Jack ring up a dance instructor to give me lessons.* However, every time I gazed about the table, Phyllis met my eye and smiled rather proudly at me. I bit my tongue.

We could stall no longer. Phyllis suggested that Lucy and I make our way into the library and prepare for the little show.

Henderson quietly directed a footman to take over for him and followed us. We found the driver pacing in the dimly lit the room. Out of uniform, he looked quite the dandy.

Quickly changed into their best frocks, the two maids slipped inside the elegant chamber. With white knuckles, they grasped their typed-out lines.

By habit, one of the little women went to turn on a lamp, and Lucy called out, "No, we just want the chandeliers on so that we can turn them off in an instant."

"The moon is casting a glow; close the curtains as well," I suggested.

Phyllis snapped the fingers of her good hand and told the chauffeur to place a comfortable chair by the light switch; she would play stagehand. The man's eyes turned to daggers. He did as she requested with flaring nostrils.

"Oh, you'll need these," Lucy said, and gave me a small box of matches.

I felt a bit flushed, and when the door leading to the hall opened, I feared I might swoon.

The two brothers and their wives joined us, fresh cocktails in their hands. They looked about and saw that the two couches had been moved; no longer facing each other, they were side by side, looking onto the long wall with the closed curtains. This was where the action would take place.

My unhappy performers clustered together, all looking down as if a spot on the carpet had mesmerized them. Nate left the side of the chair where the script had called for the fictional feline to lounge, and collapsed at Ruth's feet.

As the two couples each settled into their own couch, I stepped before them and said, "I hope you have the lowest of expectations; this is only from the first draft."

At the beginning of the week, I had thought they all looked so young for their ages. Their cattiness towards one another had seemed almost a lark. Looking at them as they stared me down with cold eyes, the four appeared quite different.

Randolph, the eldest, looked dumpy in his black tie attire. Specks of silver gave character to his lifeless, oiled hair.

Nicholas, who had seemed at one time lanky, reminded me of a man on stilts. There was little of him to fill out the legs of his black slacks or the shoulders of his jacket.

Joan, almost old enough to be my mother, looked foolish in her red satin gown that revealed too much of her. The jewelry hanging on the woman was garish, and it crossed my mind that perhaps it was the sort of costume stuff that courtesans wore, always on the hunt for a more generous man.

Ruth, hawk-like, as I have said, appeared very nervous. Strain showed clearly on her angular face. I don't know why, but I felt sorry for her.

I darted a few long steps from where I had stood; not joining my begrudged actors yet, for my character entered later in the scene, I hovered next to where Phyllis sat by the light switch. She gave me a thrilled smile that reminded me of a child watching animals doing something at a zoo that they ought not be doing in public.

Unaware of the tension in the room, Lucy took *center stage,* and cheerfully said, "*Miss X and the Case of Cupid's Misdeed.* Uncle, as we will call him, has gathered about his kith and kin so that he might make an announcement." She dropped her pitch and sounded like quite the sinister character. "But as a storm approaches, a diabolical scheme is hatched."

One of the sour maids began. "My darling," she said stiffly to the gardener, "are you sure tonight is the right time to make the announcement?"

The gardener rather fancied himself the dashing lead. He put an arm across the maid's shoulder and swept the woman to his chest, and, looking down at her startled face, he said, "There could be no better evening."

Nearly everyone in the library leapt as Lucy slapped two baking sheets together in imitation of thunder.

"What about the storm?" said the maid in a hollow voice.

"What of it?" the gardener asked dramatically.

"It has delayed your niece and that friend of hers." She sounded as if someone were standing on her foot.

"No matter. In fact, I shall tell everyone now."

The other servants had been pretending to speak amongst themselves. Ahead of cue, their mumbling fell silent.

My star called out very boldly, "Quiet, everyone. I must have your attention." They were all perfectly silent when he repeated, "Please, I say, I must have your attention."

Looking toward the couches, I noticed Nicholas watching intently, while his brother was stifling a yawn.

The gardener went on with his dialogue, "I have an announcement to make—" He stopped speaking abruptly and looked to Lucy, who slapped the baking sheets together again.

As planned, Phyllis reached over and turned the chandeliers above us off. I think I heard Ruth give a little gasp; she might have even inadvertently kicked Nate, as the normally silent dog gave a hushed yelp. Coincidentally, in my manuscript, the fictional cat screeches because his tail is stepped on by the culprit.

I quickly walked over to the table at the middle of the performance. The sound of a thud told me that the gardener had dropped to the floor as called for by my script. I hoped not to trip on him or the candlestick left on the floor.

I felt about the table, anticipating that the candelabra and a set of matches was waiting for me. My character would make a dramatic entrance by striking a match, lighting the candles one by one, thus introducing me before the victim is seen knocked down and just clinging to life.

I felt a cigarette box, then an ashtray, but I couldn't find the candelabra. The silence went on, and I became frantic about my missing prop. At last, I said, "I must break character. This is most embarrassing; I can't seem to find the candles. Phyllis, do be a dear and switch the lights back on."

There was no reply. After a second, Ruth called out, "Phyllis!"

I could hear the movement of bodies rising from the couch. Then there were footfalls behind me. The lights overhead came back on. Henderson stood at the switch, looking down on a crumpled form.

It seemed odd to me that the gardener was still prone on the floor, and far from the center of our performance. Then, my eyes focused on the extremely dark black hair, and the dark purple velvet material.

The prop that I had been searching for was on the floor next to Phyllis's lifeless body. Candles, some broken, surrounded the woman. I looked at the candelabra and thought to myself, *Et tu, Brute?*

Chapter Eight

A frantic call was placed to Ampthill; where this was located, I could not say. What felt like a long span of time passed before several police officers, or as I thought they were called there, constables, arrived.

A few uniformed men walked the grounds, while several fellows in dark suits and hats questioned the doctor, who had arrived before them.

One man in particular seemed to be in charge. As Lucy would point out once her wits had returned, he would fit nicely into the story of my manuscript. Tall and pleasant on the eye, he had wavy dark hair cut in the current fashion. His eyes were green, and his skin showed some color that indicated athletic pursuits.

Standing in the hall next to the library, this man asked Nicholas, "Does the dog bark at strangers?"

Nicholas's head swung toward Nate, and he replied, "No. I don't think he knows how to bark."

"Come again?" asked the handsome fellow.

Nicholas gave an apologetic shrug and replied, "The dog is from Kabul. I don't think they bark there."

"I should think they'd bark there more than anywhere else," said Randolph.

Joan hissed, "This isn't the time."

"What an exotic place to find a dog," remarked the policeman.

Nicholas reached down to pat Nate's head. "An unasked for gift. An acquaintance gave the idiot dog to my wife. Silly woman thought it might make for another companion after Phyllis died."

"Nicholas, what an ugly thing to say," snapped Ruth.

"I beg your pardon?" the policeman said with flaring   nostrils.

Nicholas looked to Ruth. "Well, it is true. We can say it now that she is dead." And then, to the inspector, "Phyllis had a tumor; she was dying. The breeder gave my wife the dog as a distraction."

"Phyllis was dying, you say? Then why murder her?" asked the policeman, making a note in his little book.

"Exactly!" said each couple, in unplanned unison.

Slowly, the policeman turned to face me and asked them, "Was there anyone present at the time of the crime who was unaware of Miss Masterson's terminal condition?"

They glared at me, and Ruth said, "I don't know how well informed our guests from London are."

Quickly, I admitted, "We had not a clue." The truth was, we hadn't read them right. It seemed obvious after the fact, her lack of appetite, her constant fatigue, and the way Ruth catered to her.

"You are the two guests spending the week?" asked the policeman. Nicholas had already given him the overview of the events leading up to Phyllis's death.

"Yes," I replied, not caring for the way he looked me up and down.

The policeman looked to poor Lucy and said, "You are Mrs. Stayton?"

She shook her head and pointed to me as she replied, "No. I'm Lucy Wallace."

The man's eyes narrowed as he glanced at me again, and, as if he did not believe it, he asked, "You're Mrs. Stayton?"

I nodded and watched him remove a small envelope from the pocket of his jacket. He reached out his hand, giving me the object. "Would you open the envelope?"

It had already been very carefully unsealed. I took a small piece of stationary from the matching envelope, which had my name on it.

"Please read what it says—aloud," said the policeman.

I could not but help hear Phyllis's voice as I read, "My dear child, I have wronged you. For this, I am sorry. Phyllis." I glanced up and said, "There is a postscript, a quote from the novel *Great Expectations*."

"Please read it," the policeman said.

"So, throughout life, our worst weaknesses and meannesses are usually committed for the sake of the people whom we most despise."

As I looked up from the note, I saw Ruth dab away a tear from the corner of her eye.

"What does that mean to you?" asked the policeman. His voice was uncomfortably commanding.

"I haven't the faintest idea."

"Had she wronged you in any way?" the policeman asked.

"Not at all; in fact, she had been rather kind to me," I replied.

Joan let out an ugly laugh. "Phyllis was kind to you? She thought you were a little fool; didn't you see the way she looked down her nose at you?"

I had been polite, I had been cheery, and I'd had enough. "No, Joan, I didn't notice Phyllis making any imitation of you."

Randolph snickered, Nicholas put his hand to his mouth, and Ruth's head dipped as she tried to catch sight of Joan's reaction.

Before the situation might become nasty, the policeman said, "It is very late, and you are all tired. I suggest you all get a good night's sleep, and I will meet you all in the morning."

I stepped forward. "I would like for you to question Miss Wallace and myself tonight. I intend on calling home and having the car sent for me as soon as possible." I was done with these people. I would not sleep under the same roof as a murderer.

The policeman took back the letter in my hand. He would not meet my eye as he responded, "I think not, Mrs. Stayton. After all, you are currently my chief suspect."

There was no pretense made indicating that we were still welcome guests. Coming downstairs, we found Henderson waiting for us. Apologetically, he said, "If you are hungry, a small buffet is available in the kitchen. I have set places for you on the terrace."

I thanked him graciously, and we followed him. The servants ate well enough, and we shared in their morning meal.

Lucy had tried to make some small talk, and I tried to respond, but the effort proved too much for each of us. We ate our cold scrambled eggs and toast in near silence.

"Come along," I told my dear friend as I heard a motorcar approaching from the drive.

We were just coming down the hall as Henderson was inviting the policeman, the same one who had questioned us the night before, inside.

The butler made some comment about the family still being in their rooms, and the officer nodded, and then tipped his hat to Lucy and me.

"Miss Wallace, Mrs. Stayton," he said.

"Morning," I replied.

Lucy mumbled something and clasped her hands. I felt so sorry for the poor dear.

"Come again?" he asked.

I spoke for her. "This is all such a strain on my poor friend. Might you do us the kindness of interviewing her first, and then she can get some rest."

"No need to be under a strain; I have just a few questions for you," the policeman said kindly. He looked about the entrance hall, and, seeing the bright light of the morning sun seeping past the open doors of the vacant dining room, he gestured with his hat for Lucy to enter. He closed the doors behind them, giving me an odd smile as he did so.

Henderson excused himself when he noticed that Nate was at the top of the staircase, whining. As he went to rescue the dog, a thought occurred to me.

I slipped back to the kitchen and then carefully pushed a pocket door to one side; this gave me entrance to the butler's pantry between the dining room and the kitchen. Carefully, I rolled the door back into place.

After I settled myself, I could hear the policeman speaking, "Right, tell me Miss Wallace, how do you come by your income? Are you a paid companion to Mrs. Stayton?"

"I couldn't rightly put it that way. We are the best of friends, but she doesn't so much pay me..." She trailed off.

"So you have no income," the policeman said incredulously.

"I don't need an income; I have no expenses. Of course, Mr. Jack sneaks a bit of money in my purse every week or so."

"Who is Mr. Jack?"

"The Cissy who manages the family's money," Lucy replied.

"A homosexual runs the accounts."

She stuttered, "The Stayton family wouldn't employee someone who dabbled in criminal behavior. I just mean to say that he's effeminate, you know, the kind of man who holds his cigarette like a woman, never realizing he has ash on his shoulder."

"I see," replied the policeman. Then, after a long pause, he asked her, "Tell me, Miss Wallace, do you know how Mr. Xavier Stayton died?"

"No, we've never discussed his death," Lucy responded.

"Doesn't that seem strange to you?"

"No stranger than you asking me about poor Mr. Stayton now that he's been in the family mausoleum for these past three years, at the same time there's a dead cripple still waiting to be buried at the church graveyard just down yonder," she retorted, no longer sounding so nervous.

Insulted, the policeman snapped at her, "How is it you found yourself Mrs. Stayton's companion? How did you provide for yourself before?"

Lucy had no choice but to answer the man's question. I had a choice not to listen to the answers, thus I crept out of the butler's pantry.

No more than fifteen minutes passed before Lucy and the policeman stepped back into the wide formal hallway.

The fellow's brow rose when he saw me sitting on a little upholstered bench that I had dragged there myself.

"Am I next?" I asked, squeezing Lucy's hand as she stepped next to me.

"Why not? The rest of the family doesn't seem as eager as you do." He gestured toward the open door and started to walk back inside the dining room.

I leaned in to Lucy and quickly whispered, "First, call home and have the car sent up for us. Then, speak to the staff, find out all you can. I don't care if you make fools of us, because we are leaving as soon as that man clears me of any wrongdoing."

"Mrs. Stayton," called the policeman, and I hurried in after giving Lucy a little hug of reassurance.

I sat down on a chair at the end of the table and said, "Now, Constable—"

"I'm an inspector, and you are an American," he said with a funny smirk.

"Didn't take many clues for you to deduce that, Inspector," I quipped, just as the master sleuth should.

"What brings you here, Mrs. Stayton?" he asked, ignoring my attempt to be witty.

"I came to Pearce Manor to be inspired; you see, I am writing a novel." I thought perhaps he'd be rather impressed with me.

"No, I mean, what brings you to England?"

I felt my brow wrinkle. "My husband's family is English. He lived in London." I became tongue-tied; those weren't the words I had wanted to say. I corrected myself, "I live in London."

"Your husband, he is…?" The man intentionally let his words trail off.

"With the Lord Almighty, charming the angels," I told him.

"I'm so sorry." His eyes squinted. I was fearful he'd ask the dreaded question, but instead, he inquired, "How did you two meet?"

"Xavier was an explorer, you know the sort. He wanted to see the world. He was in America, headed to California to see the 1923 World's Fair. My mother and I were at the Union Station, collecting my Great Aunt Dotty, when Xavier's train brought him to St. Louis.

"We made eyes with each other in the restaurant. He introduced himself to me—well, to my mother and me. We invited him to join us. We fell in love in that instant."

I noticed the inspector's jaw set, as if he found this hard to believe, and he said as much.

Defensively, he remarked, "You are an attractive young lady, but love at first sight? I don't know that I believe in such a thing."

"I may not be a typical temptress, but I've turned a head or two, Inspector," I assured him.

He gave me his version of the polite chuckle and then responded, "Of that, I am sure." He paused as if reexamining me before he asked, "So you met and fell in love?"

"Yes, he never left for Los Angeles. He took a room at a hotel. For the next month, he courted me and then asked my father's permission to marry me."

"What a romance," the inspector remarked.

I smiled and nodded my chin.

After a long pause, the inspector reached inside his jacket and pulled out his cigarette case. He offered one to me, and I declined. Slowly, he lit his own and took a long drag from it before saying, "Right. Now, about the evening of the murder, a manuscript that you have written was being acted out. The lights went out and...?"

"On cue, Phyllis turned off the chandelier. We heard the *thunk,* then I reached for the candelabra, but it wasn't there. Finally, I asked Phyllis to turn the light on. She didn't respond. When her name was called out and she did not reply, Henderson turned on the chandelier. Phyllis was prone on the floor, and the candelabra was on the floor beside her."

"Who called to Phyllis, besides yourself?"

"Ruth," I replied.

"Who set out the candelabra on the table?"

"I did myself."

"Where did you get it from?"

"It was always in the room," I told him.

"When I arrived, it was back on the table," he told me.

"Yes, by reflex, Henderson picked it up and replaced it."

The inspector asked, "Was he wearing gloves?"

I thought about the question for a moment. "Yes, why?"

"There were a few fingerprints on the item, I suspect yours. Otherwise, it was quite clean."

"Of course my fingerprints will be on the thing," I retorted.

"What about matches?" he asked.

"Yes, Lucy had set out a little box of matches for me to use."

"I saw no box of matches on the table last night."

I thought about it for a moment; they were also missing from the table. "Yes, I don't remember them being on the table as I reached about."

Rhetorically, he asked, "Who has them now?" then he looked to me and asked, "Were they in a large box or a small box?"

Yes, this would be an excellent clue. "A small box; it was from the Hotel Cote d' Azur. They had been in Lucy's luggage since our trip to Monte Carlo."

He smiled at me, pleased with my handy piece of information. "Had there been any tension in the house during your stay?"

"Nothing but. My husband's family are not what I would call happy people," I told him.

"And Miss Masterson?"

"She was a queer individual. I have to admit, she frightened me at first. Because of her gaunt figure and the way she held her injured arm, she seemed rather sinister. As I got to know her, though, my opinion changed."

The inspector asked, "How did she interact with the Staytons?"

"Ruth was very devoted to her. Nicholas was...respectful, friendly. I think Randolph may have spoken to her, some. Joan ignored her for the most part, or rather, they ignored each other."

"How did she get on with the servants?" he asked.

When Phyllis wanted a cigarette lit, she had relied on Ruth or Nicholas. She rarely spoke to Henderson or the maids, and she'd indicated she thought little of the chauffeur. "She treated them like nameless domestic help, neither politely nor rudely."

He made a note in his book. "Right. You've had time to think about it now. Tell me, has it occurred to you why she had that letter inside her cigarette case at the ready to give to you?"

I answered too quickly. "No."

He peered at me suspiciously and asked, "Did the two of you discuss the novel she quoted from?"

"At luncheon with the vicar's wife, she saw the book and quoted from it."

"The same quote?" he asked.

"No, though it was rather dark as well. *In a word, I was too cowardly to do what I knew was right, as I had been too cowardly to avoid doing what I knew to be wrong.* She had said that several of the passages of the book had spoken to her."

The inspector wrote down what I told him. Once his pencil was done moving, I said, "I can assure you that I had no reason to murder poor Phyllis."

The handsome man met my gaze and said, "Last night, I had the impression that your in-laws would like for me to think otherwise."

Chapter Nine

After checking in with Lucy, I hid myself in the butler's pantry once more.

I could hear Ruth speaking after I was settled with my ear against the door. "No, Randolph and Joan were away at the time. I heard her scream and went running to see what had happened."

"And what had happened?" asked the inspector.

"She'd lost her footing and tumbled down the stairs. I can't tell you how frightened I was," Ruth replied.

"This was four years ago, you said; before that, how long had she been your secretary?"

Ruth must have been calculating, as it took her a moment to reply. "Four years."

"How did she come to you?" he asked.

"She had worked for my husband's company. When he sold off his percentage, we hired her," she replied stiffly.

"So you've known her for longer than these past eight years?"

"No, I hadn't met her. While my husband was away in the war, she was his secretary in London. He realized that she'd be sacked with his departure…"

"What type of company was he a part of?"

I did not hear Ruth's reply; my heartbeat doubled as the door to the pantry from the kitchen edged open. To my relief, it was Lucy. She handed me a note and then crept away as quickly as she had appeared.

I read her hurriedly scribbled note. Thus far, Lucy had learned that Phyllis had once been very friendly with the domestic help, more one of them than part of the family. After the fall, this changed. She had become demanding of them while she convalesced and had made an enemy of the former butler, whom Henderson had replaced. This was all told by the gardener.

Putting my ear back to the door, I heard the inspector ask, "And how long did the doctor tell you she had left?"

Ruth's voice was very soft when she replied, "He'd said six months, at the longest."

"So she had maybe two, three months..."

"I doubt even that long. She had been resistant to go on morphine; she was dealing with the pain as best as she could. Still, she was getting weaker and weaker, and she hardly ate. Just the other day, I had the dress she is to be buried in sent for alterations."

I understood now why the secretive errand had been done while Phyllis was occupied.

The inspector paused for a moment before changing the line of his questioning. "Your brother-in-law, how is it that he and his wife live with you?"

"Nicky and Randolph are most loyal to each other. Randolph found himself in hard times after the war. I suppose even beforehand. Their father left them debt, not money. As the older brother, Randolph did his best to pay his father's notes; it left him in a bad way. The family home was sold for a song during the July

Crisis—Randolph has always been one to say dark little things that he believes to be humorous. He called the selling of the estate his July Crisis."

"You all get along?"

Ruth's tone was questionable. "As well as two brothers and their wives might under one roof."

"And how is that?" the inspector prodded.

"I think Randolph tires of living with his younger brother; it does raise an eyebrow or two among *our* social circle," she said, as if the inspector needed to be reminded of the class distinction between him and her.

"You get on well with your sister-in-law."

There was a long pause, too long. "We have found our way. During the war, she lived with her mother and step-father, dreadful people. At first, she seemed happy to be here, perhaps somewhat humbled. Then she started to resent us." There was another pause, and I wished that I could have seen the expression on her face. "That all changed. When she and Randolph returned from their holiday, just shortly before Phyllis's accident, she was different."

"How so?"

"Pleasant, almost grateful, she was charming as she had been when she and Randolph first married," Ruth replied in a faraway voice. After a pause, she said rather sharply, "I don't see what this has to do with Phyllis's death."

Responding to her statement, the inspector asked, "You and the deceased were close friends, as I understand. Tell me, who would have reason to harm her?"

"No one!" Ruth blurted out. Calming herself, she went on, "At least, no sane person. Isn't it obvious who did this?"

"No, who did this?" the inspector asked, slowly.

"That dammed American," Ruth told the man.

"What of her friend, Miss Wallace?"

Ruth responded, "She's a pretty little flower who sprang from a weed. I doubt she has the smarts to get out of the way from a moving car, let alone kill someone."

I heard a match strike, and after a pause, the inspector asked, "Does it take a smart person to commit a murder?"

Ruth replied, "I suppose it doesn't, just a smart person to get away with one."

"Thank you for your help. That will be all for now."

Ruth mumbled something as I heard the chairs moving. Then, the inspector made another statement. "You didn't happen to see my matches that I left here last night?"

"Matches?" she replied, sounding annoyed by the question.

"Yes, in a box from the Hotel Cote d' Azur."

"No, but I would think an inspector should be able to find them," she retorted in an ugly voice.

I heard movement in the kitchen. The little door didn't slide open, so it meant that the cook was preparing lunch, and I was trapped.

Several minutes passed before I heard Nicholas's voice. "You seem to have done a damn fine job of upsetting my wife, if that was your intent."

They settled at the table, and the inspector replied, "My apologies," in a way that sounded as if he'd been told that a great many times.

"Well, let's get on with it. Phyllis worked for me during the war; I'm sure you already know that. She handled my correspondence, and kept me *in the know,* as they say."

"Yes, your wife mentioned something like that," replied the inspector.

"Right. Well, there was more to it than she knew. I'll make no bones about it, when the war seemed to be a sure thing, I bought into a munitions company. I went off to the war, found myself in Africa, a miserable place.

"While I was there, Phyllis got wind of something, and she wrote me a letter. One of my partners was acting rather dubiously. With her help, I sidestepped what would have been rather an embarrassment."

"So you were in her debt?" asked the inspector.

"That makes it sound like I owed her something. She had done me a favor; I didn't want to see her sacked when I sold out of the company. Oh, we called her Ruth's secretary, but she was more than that. Phyllis wrote my letters, kept files, rang up appointments, all sorts of things."

"How does this play into Miss Masterson's death?"

Nicholas responded boldly, "It doesn't. I just figured you'd have questions. My brother made an ugly accusation once, that there was something between Phyllis and me, and well, there wasn't. She looked out for my best interests when I couldn't."

The inspector made what was surely meant to be an infuriating reply. "Yes, I see."

Sounding very hostile, Nicholas said, "That American is the culprit. The daffy thing is obsessed with murder; it's all she talks about. Ask her! You go ask her about her husband's death, there is a reason it's a bloody secret, I tell you."

"I peg your pardon?"

Nicholas went on, "My cousin's boy, he died mysteriously. They didn't tell us what happened to him. At the funeral, all I heard was the term, *an unfortunate accident.* Would someone like to describe a bloody accident that isn't a misfortune?"

"Right. You're saying you haven't a clue to what happened to him?"

In a voice unlike my picture of mild-mannered Nicholas, he snarled, "Not a clue."

There was a bit of silence, and then the inspector asked, "Speaking of accidents, were you injured in the war?"

"No," Nicholas snapped.

"I noticed your limp and thought perhaps…"

Nicholas gave a little grunt. "Oh, just an automobile accident." He then lowered his pitch, "Now, listen to me, none of us had reason to kill Phyllis; for Christ's sake, she was terminally ill."

"And you are convinced that Mrs. Xavier struck Phyllis at the back of the head with the candelabra."

"Who else?" Nicholas responded.

"What about this Lucy person?"

"Ms. Wallace? She hasn't the wherewithal to commit murder. Nice enough girl; I don't understand why she has gotten herself mixed up with that American."

"Do you care for a cigarette?"

Nicholas replied, "Too early; if I start now then I won't stop until the end of the evening."

"Smart," said the inspector. He paused, and then said, "You haven't seen a box of matches that I mislaid last night, have you?"

"I don't recall."

The inspector replied, "Fancy little box, had the name of Hotel Cote d' Azur on it."

"I'll keep an eye out," Nicholas said, curiously.

The shuffle of chairs began, and the inspector told Nicholas that those were all the questions he had for him at the time.

The other policeman, this one junior to him, stepped into the room, and they whispered as if my presence was known. The other man walked away briskly, and then the inspector welcomed Joan into the dining room.

"Morning, Mrs. Stayton..."

"Oh, do come to the point. I didn't much care for old Phyllis, but Mother Nature had already set to do her in, so why would I?"

"Why would anyone?" the inspector asked whimsically.

"Give me a cigarette, and I'll tell you."

There was a moment of silence, the strike of a match, and then Joan said, "That's better." There was a little pause, just enough time to take a long drag. "Tell me, what do you know about those rifles the Canadians were armed with during the war?"

The inspector made no response. I imagined that he shrugged at Joan's question.

"Maybe this will ring a bell. In wet areas, they jammed. The Canucks hated them so much that they'd pitch them on the ground and use their revolvers."

"Go on."

"You know that Phyllis was employed by Nicky during the war. I'm sure he's already pointed the finger at my Randolph, but he was just a guilty."

"I haven't a clue as to what you are saying."

Joan let out her ugly imitation of laughter. "Randolph made a deal to resell the rifles...Nicholas didn't tell you any of this?"

"I'm afraid not. Your husband and his younger brother were business partners, you say?"

Joan sounded completely different to me when she replied, "I don't think I should say any more."

"That isn't an option, Mrs. Stayton."

"Randolph was a junior partner; he was already down on his luck when the idea was cooked up. He had little to offer."

The inspector asked, "So it was he who had to do the dirty work. He managed to collect the malfunctioning rifles and transport them?"

"I don't know the details—I never asked. All that I do know is that he wasn't smart about it. He sent a letter that said too much. The other business partner, in London, dictated a stern reply."

"And Phyllis took this dictation?"

Joan's response was delayed. I could imagine her puffing from her cigarette before she spoke. "Yes. Phyllis realized what was going on." Joan gave a grunt. "The poor dear thought Nicky to be above such a thing. He and his partner cut Randolph out, thinking him too half-witted to trust."

"It sounds as if your husband might have reason to kill Miss Masterson after all."

Joan bit back, "Why? She would have been dead by the end of summer."

"Then why tell me all of this?"

"Better to hear it from me than the servants…" her voice trailed off.

"Then who might have killed Miss Masterson?"

Quickly, Joan said, "The American."

"Why?"

"Her mother-in-law put her up to it," she said, in a very thrilled tone.

"Why would she do that?" asked the inspector.

"You didn't ask me who the third partner in the munitions business was, Inspector."

"I am remiss. Who was this person?"

Joan replied triumphantly, "My husband's cousin."

"Mrs. Xavier's father-in-law?"

"The very same." She barked her laugh again and said, "He was forced to buy out Nicky, Randolph too, but there was little reward. The stress of it all was too much for him. He died one morning, they say in his bathrobe, arguing with the cook."

I wanted to burst through the door and accuse the woman of lying, but she wasn't so much lying as pontificating. These were her version of the facts.

I was startled when the door behind me jolted, but did not open. The next instant, a little slip of paper was pushed under the door. I heard Lucy's voice telling the cook, "No, I just dropped my pad. Thank you."

I skimmed her note, quickly. The old butler was fired after he made an unsavory comment about Phyllis, something about she wouldn't have taken a misstep if she wasn't always sneaking through the house.

Henderson, who had come with Randolph and Joan as a footman, took the position. He had done well to befriend Phyllis.

Most scandalous, though, was this bit of gossip: it was generally suspected that, before the accident, some sort of relationship existed between the chauffeur and Phyllis. His feelings for her waned after it became clear she would not recover. This information was a compilation of the maids' knowledge.

I thought to myself, *Why else would Phyllis suggest a spurned lover? She had been one.*

The sound of Joan's ugly, barking laughter caught my ear, and I moved back to the other side of the butler's pantry.

"Miss Wallace? My husband told me he recognized her from Xavier's funeral. She looked a vagabond at the time. Now look at her, decked out in H and K's spring wardrobe. I suspect she knows what that American did to Xavier and is blackmailing her."

The inspector said with a muffled voice, "You've been most helpful." It sounded as if he'd placed a cigarette between his lips while he spoke.

"It is a pity that people don't hang in public anymore. I'd like to see that girl dangling from a noose."

The inspector ignored Joan's mean-spirited comment and asked, "I left a box of matches here last night; you didn't happen to find it?"

"Unless it was floating in a bottle of gin, I wouldn't have been looking for it."

The chairs were shoved about, and then Joan's heels struck the floor relentlessly as she made her dramatic exit.

I heard the inspector sit back down. He began to tap his fingers on the table. Was he thinking what I was: how did I not know that my husband's father and the man's cousins had been petty war profiteers?

I was sure that Mother Stayton had no idea, or she wouldn't have let me travel to Pearce Manor. Xavier hadn't known. When I asked him where his family money came from, he'd been rather stumped by the question. He listed a slew of investments and shrugged, not all that concerned as to how the coffers were filled.

There was a sound at the door, and it seemed that Lucy had promptly returned with more information.

Then Henderson appeared; the man smiled at me and handed me a plate of lunch.

Blushing, I took the dish. He gracefully stepped back and closed the pantry door, not making a sound.

I nibbled away at a cold piece of chicken while the inspector gathered his thoughts. I was just licking my greasy fingers when the voice of the junior officer startled me. I wasn't sure how long he'd been in the room.

"Yes, that's what the vicar's wife said."

"How odd. Fetch me the older brother."

I listened to the inspector pace until Randolph entered the room. "Garish, isn't it?"

"How's that?"

Randolph scooted a chair from the table. "This room, absolutely garish."

"I thought it was rather fancy."

Randolph gave a harrumph and said, "That's what Nicky was hoping people would think."

"Are you implying something, Mr. Stayton?"

"What do you think happened to the tapestries, the oil paintings, the crystal chandeliers that used to be in these rooms?"

"I hadn't concerned myself with the décor," replied the inspector.

"Nicky sold it all—this French look, it is cheap stuff, nothing of value. No, he had a broker in London, all hush-hush, sell off the good stuff."

"And why did your brother do that?"

Randolph grunted, sounding like his younger brother. "You're the detective, you tell me?"

"Your brother's financial affairs are not what I am investigating. The murder of Miss Masterson is my concern."

"And you make to pin it on me, because I'm the failure. Well, look around, Inspector Fowler, Nicky isn't so well off either."

"Are you telling me that Nicholas murdered Miss Masterson for financial gain?"

"No, of course not. I'm just telling you, we all have our secrets."

"Such as Canadian rifles."

"I knew he'd point a finger at me..."

"Your wife was the one pointing fingers, Mr. Stayton, not your brother."

I heard the creak of a chair, as if someone had shifted their weight. "Ah, good old Joan. Did she tell you how she left me? Moved in with her mother and stepfather."

"While you were in the war?"

Randolph grunted. "It was convenient for her. When it was all over, and I hadn't anywhere to turn, she didn't ask her mother to take me in. Do you know why?"

The inspector made no reply that I could hear.

"She said, 'Go live with your brother, I have better prospects.' And she did, the little monster was trying to seduce her stepfather. Sickening, isn't it?"

No reply this time either.

"Her attempt failed, and she was packed up and put out on the street like the filth she was. Still, the little flat I had wasn't good enough for us. She told me she'd come back to me if I debased myself, crawled to my brother and got us set up here."

"And you complied."

Sounding very sorry for himself, Randolph responded, "Of course I did. I would do anything for her."

"Would you murder for her?"

Randolph gave a little laugh. "She hasn't asked me to, yet."

"Your wife went through many moods, after a bad patch, you and she returned from holiday. She was warm and gracious, for a time, then Phyllis had her accident."

"Yes, we had a row; I was mad enough that I threatened to divorce her. I lost my temper and struck her. That had never happened before. I thought she'd hit me back. She didn't; something inside her changed. She started acting the way she used to, for a time."

"You came back, and then Phyllis had her accident?"

"Just a few weeks later, yes. Of course, we were away when she took her fall, the poor dear. Talk about changed. She was never the same," Randolph said compassionately.

"Tell me how?"

"I don't know, she'd been sweet, always smiling. She adored Ruth and treated Nicky like he was some sort of hero."

The inspector asked, "After the accident, she treated them differently?"

"She and Ruth, no, the same, but now on equal footing, no longer the secretary but as a dear friend. Phyllis treated Nicky as if he wasn't so grand in her eyes anymore. She seemed jaded."

"Why do think that is?"

"I can't say; she was in pain, but she was hopeful to make a full recovery. It was an emotional time. My insight is also hindsight. At the time, I wouldn't have thought what I think now."

The inspector asked, "And what do you think now?"

Randolph lowered his voice. "I am not so sure her fall down the stairs was an accident."

"An attempt to harm her?"

Sounding more like himself, he grunted and said, "Harm her? Have you looked at those stairs? More like an attempt to murder her."

"Do you have a culprit in mind?"

"No," Randolph replied with little conviction.

"Mr. Stayton, your wife was on her best behavior for a time; when did that change?"

Randolph seemed to think about the question for some time before he answered, "A month or so later, about the time of Nicky's accident."

"His motorcar accident?"

"That's what he calls it. He was in town, and a drunk ran over his foot when he was leaving the pub. The fool drove off and left him there in the road."

"Was anyone with him?"

"No. I was away at a reunion, or I would have been with him."

"Where was his wife?" asked the inspector.

"She'd taken Phyllis to see a specialist in London," replied Randolph.

The inspector did not ask my question, *Where was Joan?* Instead, he said, "What about Mrs. Xavier, do you think she has anything to do with this?"

"Oh no, a daffy creature, but sweet enough. Have you put your eyes on that Miss Lucy? Beautiful girl."

The inspector ignored his comment. "Care for a cigarette?"

"Not a bad idea."

There was a pause, and the inspector asked, "You haven't come across a box of matches I left last night, have you? It's from the Hotel Cote d' Azur?"

"Oh, yes, *Monty*. No, I can't say that I have," Randolph replied.

"Thank you; you have been quite helpful," said the inspector. I rather disagreed. Randolph had spouted out all sorts of random information, but nothing seemed clearer to me.

Chapter Ten

The cook and the chauffeur were both interviewed by the inspector, but neither had much information that was new to me. The chauffeur had indeed been in a secret but short-lived love affair with Phyllis, but according to him, she had ended the relationship, not him.

Both servants spoke freely in regards to Randolph and Joan, but were reserved when asked questions about Nicholas and Ruth.

After speaking to these two, the other policeman joined the inspector. I could not hear what the junior man said, only the inspector's response. "Yes, that is rather strange. Send in the butler."

A few minutes later, I heard Henderson's voice, "Good day, sir."

"Please, have a seat."

"Thank you, Inspector Fowler."

"At the time of Miss Masterson's death, where were you?"

"I was quite nearby. As you know, we were acting out Mrs. Xavier's manuscript."

"Have you any opinion on who might have struck the victim?"

There was a long pause before Henderson replied, "I'm afraid I am of no help to you."

"How long have you been with the Stayton family?"

"A number of years, sir. I started with Mr. Randolph and Mrs. Joan; I was their butler. They let go of their staff shortly before the war. I was fortunate enough to be hired on by Mrs. Joan's stepfather. He took me on as a footman. It was a reduction, but I was happy for the job. As I'm sure you have already found out, there was some ugliness, and Mrs. Joan moved out of the house. I tendered my resignation, and shortly, I came here in the same capacity."

"How long have you been the butler here?" asked the inspector.

"Let's see. The previous butler was terminated…"

"For something he said about Miss Masterson."

"Indeed," Henderson responded.

"Was his comment true?"

"I wouldn't know, sir," Henderson replied in a way that said his predecessor had misspoken, but had not lied.

"You are very much the eyes and ears of the house. Is there anything that you would like to share with me?"

"Only that there is much tension in the house. Miss Masterson's health was a great concern. What you are seeing of the Stayton family is not typical. They are a quiet and kind family, sensible people."

"Indeed," the inspector replied, and then asked, "Do you have a light?"

"Of course, sir."

"Thanks. I left my box of matches here last night. I can't remember where."

"Yes, Mr. Nicholas mentioned that to me. I looked for them, but I haven't found them."

After a moment, the inspector replied, "Yes, thank you. That will be all."

Carefully, Henderson pushed back his chair and then came the soft, dignified sound of his footfalls.

The maids would be brought in next, and I wondered what gossip they might know. However, before they were called in, the door to the butler's pantry opened, and the inspector asked me, "Well, have you figured out who killed Phyllis?"

I shrugged and said, "Apparently, I must have committed the crime."

The handsome man stood back and gestured for me to take a seat at the table. I could tell that he was amused rather than irritated by my eavesdropping.

He sat down after I did, and his eyes lingered on me for a moment before inquiring, "Were you privy to the dealings of your father-in-law and his cousins?"

"No, Mother Stayton mentioned that Randolph had narrowly avoided some scandal after the war. That's the most that was ever said in that regard. I knew they disliked her; now I know why."

"Right. And your husband never discussed this with you either?"

"Never. It wasn't the sort of thing he'd talk about," I responded.

"There seems to be some mystery shadowing your husband's death, as I'm sure you overheard. Would you please explain the circumstances that have been kept from his family?"

I felt my soft, warm face turn into a cold ceramic mask, and I replied, "My husband was an explorer. A very brave, adventurous type, you know the sort. He went off to Ecuador, and sailing down the Amazon River, he was captured by headhunters. Need I tell you more?" I closed my eyes and put my hand to my chin before uttering, "To this day, even just the sight of a man with a small head sends me into hysterics."

The inspector began to laugh until my icy stare silenced him. Hesitantly, the inspector asked, "You are joking, are you not, Mrs. Stayton?"

"Shouldn't you be asking me about Phyllis's death rather than my poor Xavier's horrible demise?"

Not sure if he should be ashamed of himself, or furious with me, he asked, "This play you wrote, who had read it? Who knew when the lights were to be turned off?"

"Phyllis, Henderson, the maids, the cook, the gardener, and the chauffeur," I told him curtly.

"Did they memorize their lines?" he asked.

"No, well, almost, but they still had typed notes."

"They had typed sheets of paper?" he asked quizzically.

"Yes," I responded.

"Then where are they?"

I thought about the question and had no answer. "I don't know."

He nodded slowly. Before he could say anything, there was a knock on the door. "Yes?" he called.

Henderson opened the door and said quite formally, "A car has arrived for Mrs. Xavier and Miss Lucy."

I responded quickly, "Thank you, Henderson; will you see to it that our things are brought down?"

His eyes went to the inspector, who gave him a quick nod. He then replied, "Of course, Mrs. Xavier."

Once the door was closed, the inspector said rather sternly, "I haven't dismissed you."

119

"Then you shouldn't have nodded your consent to Henderson," I retorted.

"Why the rush to leave?"

Had I been the type to bark out a bit of fake laughter, his question would have been ripe for that sort of response. "I'm not welcome here, and there is a murder afoot. You can reach me and Lucy in London, but I've told you all I know."

"You haven't told me everything you know. I find it strange that a young woman tells lies about her husband's death...no, not just strange, but suspicious."

"My husband's death has no bearing on this case..."

"A woman keeping the details of one untimely death a secret was one of only two people who didn't know that Miss Masterson was dying at the time she was killed. My superiors would question my sanity after they read such a report, such a report that stated I let her leave the county."

"Extortion is it? I tell you my tragedy and you let me leave?" I asked, my tone laced with venom.

He only nodded and then lit another cigarette.

"I told you that my husband was an explorer..."

"So you told me, the vicar's wife, and that nice couple on the train."

I was impressed that his minion had found out about those two occurrences. "Indeed. However, he only made his way so far as Saint Louis, Missouri. We met, fell in love, and he brought me to his home, to his family. Everything was perfect. Our marriage was a success. We were very much in love, but he had kept a secret from me."

The inspector flicked his ash into a little dish that I had thought was silver, but, on closer inspection, I saw that it was tin.

"Less than a year after we were married, I discovered his secret. Xavier found me reading in our room, and he told me he was going to take a bath. How he luxuriated in his baths, or so I thought. I gave him a kiss and told him I might take a nap.

"More than an hour passed, and I woke. The sound of running water from the bathroom concerned me. I knocked at the door, and there was no reply.

"The butler broke down the door, Mother Stayton and I standing behind him. Xavier was in his dressing robe, crumpled on the floor, blood drying at his forehead."

The inspector made as if he was going to fish out a cigarette for me from his pocket. I stopped, gathered myself, and went on.

"Mother Stayton went into hysterics, calling out her pet name for Xavier, *my towheaded boy,* but you see, he wasn't."

The inspector's eyes narrowed, and his forehead wrinkled. "He wasn't?"

"No, I saw a little glass bowl and a comb in the sink, and there was an unfamiliar paste that had splattered on the vanity and the sink as well; it smelled so strongly that my eyes burned."

"I don't understand," admitted the inspector.

"After Xavier's toddler years, his pale blonde hair started to darken. Mother Stayton began washing his hair herself, with what she called a special shampoo, and then, when he was too old for that, she made him part of the secret. He was a brunette."

The inspector blew out a puff of smoke and looked at me as if I were a raving lunatic.

I explained, "There had been a chill in the air, so Xavier didn't open the window when he went into the bathroom to secretly bleach his roots. He was overcome by the ghastly vapors of the concoction; he passed out and struck his head on the marble bath."

The inspector started to smile, then frowned. "Another lie…"

"No, Inspector, the ugly, sad truth." I said this in a way that convinced him. "It had mattered so much to his mother, his pale, angelic hair, and then it mattered to him, because he prized his mother's pride."

"I am sorry," said the inspector, slowly, hesitantly.

"As am I. It was not a death befitting him. Xavier should have seen the world, as he wanted to, and if he fell off Mount Vesuvius, or was eaten by an alligator, or sailed into a waterfall, at least he would have made it to that exotic place and died the death of an adventurer."

I felt the first tear welling up in my eye.

"I didn't mean to upset you," said the inspector, apparently not immune to the tears of a young widow.

"Are you charging me with the murder of Phyllis Masterson, or am I free to go?" My voice cracked as I asked the question.

"If you leave, I may not solve this case," he told me.

I stood and said, "You're a better detective than that. Good day, Inspector Fowler."

Once outside of the dining room, I rubbed the tears from my face. Lucy and Henderson were waiting for me by the door. My friend handed me my purse. As I reached inside the bag for a handkerchief, Henderson kindly pulled his from a pocket of his jacket and gave it to me.

"Thank you, Henderson," I managed to say, and whisked past him, never so happy to see Mother Stayton's dark blue sedan waiting outside.

Our driver opened the door, and I found Mother Stayton waiting inside the car. Lucy gracefully followed me, and the door was closed.

My mother-in-law took one look at me and started to reach for the flask she kept in her purse.

"No, no, I'm fine," I assured her. This was, of course, a lie.

"You look very upset. I take it you liked that Miss Masterson very much," she remarked, not having the faintest idea of what had made me cry.

The car lurched forward as I nodded; it was easier to agree.

Mother Stayton could plainly see that I was a world away, so she began asking Lucy about the murder. I watched Pearce Manor from the rear window, growing smaller and smaller as we sped down the drive. Rounding onto the road, the row of tall trees obscured my view, but not my uncertainties.

The two continued to speak, but it was just noise to me, like ducks quacking in a pond.

I had to stop myself from thinking about Xavier, lifeless on the cold tile floor; that ghastly paste dried about his cowlick.

My thoughts could only be shifted to Phyllis, and her crumpled form. I spoke out loud, not in full possession of my wits, "Lucy, what happened to the sheets of typed paper that the servants held with their lines?"

Her pretty face froze, and she thought about my question. "I don't know?"

Mother Stayton asked, "This play, it was your novel?"

I didn't respond quickly enough, so Lucy said, "Yes."

"How far into the play did you get?"

Lucy answered, "Not far at all; the actual murder happened before the fictional attempted murder…"

Lucy's words caught my attention. "Yes, the attempted murder was to be acted out for them to see, for them to ponder."

My dear friend then said, "They'll never know the story. Well, unless they buy your book."

That was the point of killing Phyllis. The plot had been her idea, and the performance had been her idea. She and my story had been silenced. Whatever reaction would have taken place to my story would have caused repercussions; this was why Phyllis had written me the letter. Perhaps we would have been expelled from the house, and she would have handed me the note in the chaos of our things being collected.

I was startled by my epiphany. I reached into my handbag and found my little silver snuff box. With shaking hands, I took a clove and placed it on my tongue. As I replaced my sentimental item, my fingers touched something rough.

"I knew this trip was a mistake; they dislike us so," said Mother Stayton.

"Why is that?" asked ever-curious Lucy.

"A failed business venture during the war. I hate to mention it." However, she had our ear and loved to share a bit of gossip, so she continued, "My husband was convinced by his cousins to put out some money and buy into a munitions company before the start of The Great War. He partnered with them, and it turned out they were cheats.

"Nicholas was smart; he folded when he found out that his brother had taken on an unsavory silent partner of his own to redistribute some faulty weapons.

"Once Mr. Stayton put the pieces together, he paid back the cousins' money and simply folded the business; he was ashamed of what they'd done. It was a great financial loss to us.

"Strangely, shortly before his death, he received an extortion letter. I had forgotten all about it," Mother Stayton concluded, a little surprised by the omission from her memory.

"Extortion!" I exclaimed, as Lucy clapped her hands in shock.

"I forgot all about it, yes. The letter had threatened to expose the misdeeds that had been committed. My husband wouldn't be bullied. Rather than paying the price demanded, he left his own letter in the assigned place; he explained that he had nothing to hide."

Lucy remarked, "How brave."

Mother Stayton smiled. "He figured the threat came from Randolph's henchman; the man would have to expose himself to prove his claim."

Lucy asked, "What happened?"

"Nothing. Well, my poor dear husband died six weeks later." Mother Stayton gave a little pout.

"So there were four people who knew about these misdeeds," Lucy began.

"No, five knew—Phyllis." I reached into my purse and plucked the matchbox that I had found.

Mother Stayton, who did not understand the significance, remarked, "The Hotel Cote d' Azur; you two had such a lovely time in Monte Carlo. Now *there* is the setting for a thrilling book."

I tapped at the glass separating us from the driver and called out, "Turn back!"

Chapter Eleven

"Henderson, call the entire household to the library. Please tell them that Inspector Fowler wishes to speak to them," I said as I passed through the door.

"Yes, Mrs. Xavier," he answered with a bow, before colliding with Lucy. "My pardon, Miss Wallace."

She cocked her head to one side and smiled kindly. "My fault."

As he turned to close the door, I imagined he was surprised to see Mother Stayton sitting in the back of the sedan, taking a swig of whiskey from her flask.

Lucy and I sped toward the dining room, and the inspector and his minion stepped out of the chamber; the handsome man couldn't help but smile.

"You've had a change of heart?"

"No, I've solved the case." Hearing Joan's irritated voice from the top of the stairs, I took the inspector by the elbow and pushed him back out of sight.

Hurriedly, I explained my reckoning. The man wasn't convinced; still, he ordered his junior officer to take the back stairs and check out my hypothesis, Lucy on his tail.

Once alone, he said, "What you are asking of me is damned unorthodox. This isn't one of the books you write."

"Actually, I've never written a book. I'm still working on the first draft of my manuscript—and I realize now, there are many plot holes."

Though not as dashing as my Xavier, the inspector did have a handsome smile. He gazed at me for a moment, a moment that was a little too long. I realized that I was this man's type of girl. Pretty enough in my own right, but I was not a Hollywood starlet out of his reach. His attraction to me was a weakness. He'd hurt me, too; he'd seen me cry, and this gave me the leverage I needed. Against his better judgment, he'd already made up his mind. "What if you are wrong?"

"I'm not." I said this like the leading lady who had started off shy and unsure, but had weathered both a struggle with a greater force, and a struggle with herself.

From the dining room, we listened to them all file into the library, the scene of the crime. We waited a moment and then joined them. The inspector entered the elegant chamber first, and for a moment, I went unseen.

Nicholas's voice thundered, "What's this about?"

Then Joan spoke after laying eyes on me. "I thought she was gone; the guilty person run off."

Lucy appeared from the other door beside the fireplace and gave me a nod before slipping away again.

The inspector shook his head. "I don't believe she's the guilty person, Mrs. Joan."

Joan crossed the room and poured herself a drink from the bar cart. Everyone else sat down; Nate reclined at Ruth's feet.

Nicholas grunted and said, "Come to the point; if one of us killed Phyllis, then drag her away."

Both Ruth and Joan exclaimed, "Her!"

Randolph giggled and said, "My money is on the dog."

The servants, all standing at attention, watched the farce nervously.

"I shall come to the point, Mr. Stayton. Tell me, how long have you been paying a blackmailer?" asked the inspector.

"How dare you ask such a thing?" Nicholas replied.

"You sold off a great deal of valuables recently." The inspector pointed toward the other rooms. "You masked this by redecorating, but you came out the better."

"What of it?" Nicholas retorted.

"Why did you need the funds?"

"I have a son at Eton, and I'm paying my nephew's way as well. Times are hard; I am sure you know that, Inspector."

"Oh, yes, I do. I'm busiest during hard times."

Nicholas let out a sigh of exasperation. "I wasn't being blackmailed. My wife and I have also spent a great deal of money on Miss Masterson's various doctors."

The inspector nodded slowly. "Yes, she had done you favor, and you were in her debt."

"I don't care for the inference."

"I'm sure." The inspector paused, then, dropping his pitch, he said, "She knew quite a lot about your business, all the shady dealings with those Canadian rifles."

"I've explained that—"

"What the devil is he talking about?" Ruth's shrill voice startled Nate.

"Had she fallen down the stairs, and died, that secret would have been safely kept—" the inspector began to say.

Nicholas leapt to his feet, sending the dog scampering across the room. "Damn you! Damn you, I had nothing to do with her fall. It was an accident!"

"I don't think so, Mr. Stayton. It was the first attempt on her life, a failed attempt on her life as parodied in Mrs. Xavier's manuscript."

Ruth stood. She clasped her husband's arm and bit back at the inspector, "My Nicholas had nothing to do with her fall!"

The inspector shook his head. "No, ma'am, that's not true. He pushed her down the stairs. She lived, and he made a bargain with the devil—"

Randolph finally came to his younger brother's defense. "Balderdash! You have been reading too many of those tiresome whodunits yourself. Why would my brother kill a woman who was dying?"

"She had a change of heart. A deathbed confession was to come. Phyllis could no longer be trusted to take her knowledge to the grave," the inspector railed.

Nicholas dropped to the couch. "No," he said dumbly.

The inspector replied, "Yes, a judge will see through all your protests, and you'll hang for this…"

Ruth clutched at her blouse and groaned. "My husband didn't push Phyllis. She wasn't blackmailing him!"

The inspector shook his head, but said nothing.

Ruth stifled a sob. "He wasn't anywhere near Phyllis or the stairs; we'd had a fight, a violent fight, and he was locked in our room."

"What was the fight over, Ruth?" the inspector baited the woman.

"I was mad at Nicky!" she said, her face red.

"Why!" the inspector demanded.

She looked to her husband and said, "He smelled of a woman's perfume, and he refused to explain himself."

All eyes were on Ruth, and she fell silent and trembled.

The inspector asked Nicholas, "You were locked in your room, while your wife was in a rage and Miss Masterson was injured?"

Nicholas reeled toward the woman and bellowed, "You didn't!"

"I smelled the scent on her, and I lost my temper. It was an accident...an accident..." Ruth broke down, sobbing.

Nicholas stood like a statue, dumbfounded. He was unable to reach out to his wife, despite her need.

Randolph and Joan remained silent, cautiously watching the drama, as did the domestics.

It had been obvious to me that Nicholas hadn't known that Phyllis's fall wasn't an accident or he never would have made the tasteless little joke about them both being cripples.

Ruth began to babble. "Phyllis pleaded with me to believe her. She'd never do anything to harm me, she told me over and over. But I was sure I had smelled perfume on Nicky—I was sure." Ruth choked on her saliva. After catching her breath, she said, "Even after I had hurt her, she promised she hadn't betrayed me."

Ruth reached out to her husband. "She kept my secret."

At last, Nicholas took his wife's hand and pulled her to his side; he then lifted his other hand and pointed to Joan. "She kept her secret as well."

Randolph took a nervous step forward, and his wife held out her arm, as if to block his way.

"Careful, little brother." Randolph's words carried little weight.

Nicholas looked to his wife and said, "I should have told you when you confronted me…it was Joan's perfume."

"Served the bitch right for sneaking into my room. I tossed out a brand new bottle of Coco's best when I figured out what had happened."

"Joan!" Randolph actually attempted to cup his wife's mouth with his hand.

She shoved him away. "I'd lost my hold over Randolph. I thought perhaps Nicky might prefer a livelier partner than his cold reptile of a wife."

Randolph clutched at Joan's arm. "You've said enough!"

The hot-tempered woman continued in her diatribe to the inspector. "I tried to seduce him, but he was a coward. He shrank from the challenge, but what of it? I'll tell you right now, I didn't kill Phyllis, so don't start with your accusations."

At last, I spoke, "You had every reason to. Not only did Phyllis know why Nicholas smelled of perfume, and who the scent had belonged to, she knew you tried to run him down with your car."

I heard the maids gasp. Joan's skin flushed.

The inspector chided me, "I'll take it from here, Mrs. Xavier."

132

I bowed my head in deference to him and stepped back beside Henderson. Ever so excited, my heart raced.

"Mr. Nicholas, can you confirm this accusation that your sister-in-law is the person who attempted to run you down?"

Nicholas's mouth moved, but nothing came out; he tried again, and faintly, came the word, "Yes."

Joan ripped her arm away from her husband and swallowed what remained of her drink.

Nicholas admitted, "She followed me into town and waited for me outside of the pub. She'd had quite a bit to drink. I told her it was no good, nothing was going to happen between us. I left her, started to go to car, and then she came bowling toward me. I managed to get out of the way, except for my foot."

Shocked by this, Ruth asked, "Why didn't you tell me?"

"I couldn't have; we would have had to put her out. What would Randolph have done, forced to choose us or her?" Nicholas shrugged. "The following day, I sat Joan down, and we came to an understanding. The incident was put aside for the sake of the family."

"My noble little brother always at my rescue, bloody fool," Randolph remarked rather meekly, despite his choice of scornful words.

"You had every reason to kill Miss Masterson." The inspector directed this statement to Joan.

She barked her ugly laugh. "You just told Nicky that a moment ago."

"You've proven yourself capable of attempted murder," the inspector remarked.

Ruth put a finger in the air and said in a frail voice, "A spurned lover attempts to kill the man who refused her…that was the stupid point of the book."

I couldn't help myself. "The plot device was Phyllis's idea. Acting it out in front of you all was her idea too."

Ruth's voice became more forceful. "She was going to expose you at last, in her own way, but you stopped that from happening."

"Don't be an idiot," Joan hissed back.

Ruth rushed toward the woman, clenching her fists to strike. The brothers rushed forward before the confrontation could begin.

Randolph shouted at the inspector, "This is madness! Look what you've done."

"What *he's* done?" shrieked Ruth. "Joan has caused this all. It's because of her that I pushed Phyllis down the staircase. She tried to kill Nicky…she's the Devil incarnate!"

Joan's answer of laughter didn't sound so smug, but rather frightened. She managed some sarcasm as she scoffed, "After the inspector left last night, I thought we all agreed to blame the American; how quickly you all turn on a woman."

The inspector flashed me a brief glance. I took a nervous breath and reached into the handbag that I clutched.

Pulling out the cigarette holder that Xavier had given me, I smashed a fag into the seldom-used item with shaking hands. Then I leaned into Henderson, who was watching the family he served fall apart. Noticing my actions, he patted down his pockets and pulled out a box of matches.

He struck one against the box. He was just about to pass the lit object closer to me when his eyes caught the printing. A tremor ran through him, and I stepped back, fearful he might burn my face.

The inspector reeled around. "Is that my box of matches, old man?"

"No," said Henderson, his face contorted. "They're Miss Lucy's."

"Oh, how is it you have them?" asked the inspector; his tone was very even, almost gentle.

Henderson's eyes darted from side to side. He stammered for a moment before replying, "Miss Lucy brushed into me, entering the door. She must have put them in my pocket."

"Why?"

"How would I know? Obviously, Mrs. Xavier put her up to the act to incriminate me," he rebutted.

The inspector narrowed his eyes. "And how would a box of matches from the Hotel Cote d' Azur incriminate you?"

"They were the matches that you were looking for," Henderson replied.

All eyes were on the butler.

"Yes, and I ask again, how would the presence of this match box on you be incriminating?"

Nicholas blurted out, "What's this all about?"

I would not let the inspector take this cake. "Phyllis's murderer needed as much time in complete darkness as possible, to strike her over the head and step back to where he had been. While the candelabrum was the murder weapon, the matches must have been removed so that I couldn't use the smaller candlestick that had been the maid's prop." I paused for effect and then turned to Henderson. "This way, Henderson had time to retrace his steps and be heard striding toward the light switch, after he had killed Phyllis."

The guilty man bowed his head. "I misjudged you, Mrs. Xavier, and for that, I do apologize."

Ruth was utterly lost. "Why?"

On cue, Lucy pushed through the little door beside the fireplace. The junior policeman was behind her, holding a metal lockbox that had been pried open.

She proudly said, "Henderson's attempt to extort Mrs. Xavier's father-in-law, which, of course, none of you knew about, hadn't worked. All he had was this job, and the hope that the family fortune might rebound so he could try to put the screws to Randolph again."

The inspector took the metal box and thumbed through the papers. He looked to Randolph and showed him a faded letter. "Your instructions on selling the abandoned rifles to another munitions house?"

(I do hate when clues are flung out by writers at the very last of a whodunit; it is quite unfair to the reader. However, until Lucy had poked her head into the library just earlier, I had not known for certain that Henderson had been Randolph's legman during the war. However, I knew that he was guilty of killing Phyllis because of the box of matches that had made their way into my handbag, an item that Henderson had handed to Lucy. Just as he'd explained, Lucy thought nothing of him handling my purse, as he had seen to having our belongings taken to the foyer. I will allow the editor to drop what he believes to be the right hint ahead of time, as long as the suggestion does not give way to the conclusion.)

Randolph ripped the letter from the hand of the inspector, and he shouted at Henderson, "You kept these, these damning pieces of evidence? What kind of fool are you?"

Nicholas lost his wits. "Henderson was your dirty partner? You brought him into my home! You deceived me?"

Ruth came straight to the point, "Henderson, explain yourself."

The man knew he was caught, so he gave a little shrug and said, "Yes, ma'am. As your guests have surmised, Miss Masterson wanted a clear conscience before the eternal slumber, or perhaps nothing so noble. It seemed all that mattered was that Joan was found out by Ruth for what she had done, and caused.

"I can't say why, but she couldn't tell you herself. Thus, she found a way to get Mrs. Xavier to do so. This was all told in the little pantomime of a scorned woman who went seeking vengeance on the man who turned her away.

"I read the lines, and they were so reminiscent of the talk after Mr. Nicholas's accident. Every word the culprit said sounded as if Joan had given dictation to Miss Wallace as she typed."

The inspector asked, "You killed her to stop the performance and to silence her?"

"Indeed. It seemed so very convenient. I couldn't have Mrs. Joan found out for her brazen attack on Mr. Nicholas. She would be thrown to the curb, and Mr. Randolph would follow. I had come with them, so I suspected, I would be expelled as well, as I had been when Mrs. Joan made advances on her stepfather. A man such as myself, in his middle fifties, with a bad record of his conduct in the war, and angry former employers, has little chance of finding employment as comfortable as this."

Incredulous, the inspector asked, "You killed Miss Masterson over a job?"

Henderson, still behaving ever so properly, frowned and replied, "Not a job, young man, my entire way of life."

The inspector's expression suggested he still didn't understand the man's motive. He was too young to realize that comfort and security could be just as motivating as greed or lust.

I asked, in a strangely kind voice, "How did you know that Joan was the one who tried to run down Nicholas?"

"She returned home, quite drunk, before the hospital rang and I found out about Mr. Nicholas's injury. The following morning, I spied on her as she checked the French roadster. She showed little surprise in regards to her brother-in-law's misfortune; however, she seemed most concerned that the motor car was unharmed." Henderson gave Joan a sly smile.

"You knew the truth about Ruth causing Phyllis's accident too, didn't you?" I asked.

"Oh, yes, of course, Mrs. Xavier. Before it happened, Ms. Phyllis had been loyal and dutiful to Mrs. Ruth. Afterward, it was Ruth who became loyal and dutiful to Ms. Phyllis."

I had but one more question. "Henderson, why did you put the match box that Inspector Fowler had asked you about into my handbag?"

The man smiled at me and said, "I knew they were not his, that they were Miss Wallace's. As you surmised, it stood to reason that the murderer took them." He paused and tilted his head to one side, and rather sadly, he went on, "Had they been found on you, as I had intended, it would have been rather incriminating. You see, this time, I had hoped that the foreign red herring would, how is it that one in your profession puts it—*hang*."

Henderson gave me a polite little smile, nodded his head, and crossed the room to where the inspector stood.

Epilogue

Lucy and I stood on the other side of the street from the prison house. We did our best to blend in with the locals of Bedford.

I was rather sad for these people; for them, the execution of a complete stranger had been reason enough to deviate from their typical morning.

Would the gent beside me tell his employer he was late to work just so he could listen to the prison bell ring, and watch as an official tacked up the notice of death? Perhaps he might. Henderson's trial had nearly shut down the town.

The papers had called the story *The scandal at Pearce Manor.* Reporters trekked all the way to Holland Park to interview me. I was referred to, of course, as *Mrs. X.*

While I had testified at the trial, Lucy proved herself the true sleuth. She found out that Joan had moved into a lodge in nearby Luton. Randolph had stayed on with his younger brother and sister-in-law. Nicholas was already working with a solicitor, and the estate was on the market. Rumor had it, they intended to move to where Ruth's family resided.

Now the day had come. What those who had gathered around the prison to hear, happened. Lucy grasped my hand as the prison bell was struck.

The man beside me whispered in an eerie voice, "For whom the bell tolls."

Lucy glanced at him and then recited Mr. John Donne's poem, in her lovely English accent. *"No man is an island, entire of itself. Each is a piece of the continent, a part of the main. If a clod be washed away by the sea, Europe is the less. As well as if a promontory were. As well as if a manner of thine own or of thine friend's were. Each man's death diminishes me, for I am involved in mankind. Therefore, send not to know for whom the bell tolls, it tolls for thee."*

A few of those around us clapped their hands; others gaped awkwardly, puzzled by what they had heard. Some walked on, so it seemed the sound of the bell was enough.

As the crowd thinned, I saw Ruth and Nicholas across the street, near the prison. Both were dressed in black. The poor befuddled Afghan hound was at their side, with a black collar around his neck.

Twenty minutes passed, the prison door opened, and a hefty man in a drab suit stepped out with a uniformed officer. In a clumsy manner, each in the other's way, they managed to tack the death notice to the door.

I looked to Ruth; she leaned into her husband as some of the spectators gave a perverse cheer for the execution of man they had never met.

Never seeing me, Nicholas raised his hand into the air as he led his wife to the curb. Their dark limousine pulled forward and stopped.

From inside the car, Randolph swung the rear door open and helped his sister-in-law to the backseat. Nicholas had to scoop up the large dog and shove him in.

The family bond was unbroken, it seemed. Randolph had brought his brother's home such trouble. His wife had been the root cause of Ruth's rage and Phyllis's injury. His partner-in-crime had been a murderer. However, blood was thicker, as they say.

Distracted, I was quite surprised when a familiar voice said, "Where are your notebooks, ladies? You'll want to describe poor Ruth's reaction to the execution. How she sobbed in memory of her crippled secretary."

I could smell alcohol on Joan's breath. She had been pretty to me, before. Gazing on her at this time, she looked wretched. Her skin was pale and dry. Her eyes were bloodshot and tired. The dress she wore had been expensive, but it showed wear.

I recalled Joan had made a remark about Lucy looking a vagabond at Xavier's funeral. She looked little better now.

A confession must be made. I did not care for Dickens's novel that Ruth had quoted from, but a few words did come to mind. I spoke them aloud, *"And could I look upon her without compassion, seeing her punishment in the ruin she was."*

Joan frowned. "What is that supposed to mean?"

"Henderson paid the price for the crimes you began, but I pity you all the same."

She'd had enough to drink, this by eight o'clock in the morning, that my statement confused her. "You Americans never make sense to me."

I made no reply. The woman took a few steps away and then swung her head back over her shoulder. "I hope you publish your damned book. I shall then sue you for slander." Her ugly bark of a laugh lingered longer than she did.

A few people had remained to watch our curious exchange. I heard a woman whisper, "That's Mrs. X."

I opened my handbag and took a clove from my little snuffbox before giving Lucy a tug of the elbow. We then walked back to the car park.

There was the inspector, waiting for us. He tipped his hat and smiled. We continued walking toward the motorcar that the handsome man leaned against.

"Beautiful automobile," he said, rather than greeting us.

I gazed at the white roadster. I had to admit that I owed my ability to drive it to Joan and agreed, "Yes. It is my husband's."

"The one he was driving on the Galapagos Islands when that giant hawk swooped down and caught him?"

I gave the inspector the faintest of smiles and replied, "Had it not been for that massive tail feather stuck to the spare tire, we would never have puzzled out what had happened."

The man grinned at me, rather bashfully. "Right. Why did you make the drive all the way out here?" he asked.

"I wanted to see it through, to the end," I replied.

The inspector nodded. "Have you finished your novel?"

"I have but the last page to write."

(Here, Lucy suggests that I omit her from the conclusion and write some romantic ending; such as the handsome Inspector Fowler gazed into my eyes and told me my beauty was only second to my detective abilities. He takes me by the hands, draws me into his arms, and kisses me with much passion. However, this ending did not happen, nor does it suit the character of *Miss X*.)

"You were waiting to finish your whodunit in case you found out Henderson's last words?" the inspector said intuitively.

Hopeful, I asked, "Indeed. Do you know what his last words were?"

Sparing dear Lucy, we were all at fault. Phyllis had held the truth, but had a change of heart. Ruth had lost her temper and done a terrible thing, Nicholas and his brother had made the worst decisions, and Joan had been heartless.

Henderson had done what he thought he must, but my actions, innocent as they were, had stoked coal into the engine that he fought to derail. I hoped he had said something that might absolve me of my secret guilt, something proving his actions were his own.

"Yes, I do," said the inspector. "He was being led to the gallows, and he gave a queer chuckle before saying, 'I'll be damned, that daffy American will end her trite little book with the words, *The butler did it*.'"

Author's Notes

My thanks to Tammy, Maggie, Melissa
And, of course, Dana.

Set a course for deception when next we meet our
heroines on the high seas.

1st Class has never been so dangerous…

MURDER MOST POSH

A Mrs. Xavier Stayton Mystery

Made in the USA
San Bernardino, CA
11 September 2014